This book, like everything I do, is for Tonia and the boys.

Outlaw Biker

Outlaw Biker

THE RUSSIAN CONNECTION

JERRY LANGTON

WILEY

John Wiley & Sons Canada, Ltd.

DISCLAIMER: What follows is an attempt to describe outlaw motorcycle gang and organized crime life by using composite characters and fictional events that do not represent real people.

Library and Archives Canada Cataloguing in Publication Data

Langton, Jerry, 1965–
    Outlaw biker : the Russian connection / Jerry Langton.

Sequel to: Biker.
ISBN 978-0-470-68153-4

978-0-470-96339-5 (ePDF); 978-0-470-96341-8 (Mobi);
978-0-470-96340-1 (ePub)

    1. Mafia—Russia—Fiction. 2. Mafia—Europe, Eastern—Fiction. 3. Motorcycle gangs—Fiction. I. Title.

PS8623.A54O98 2011   C813'.6   C2010-907687-7

Production Credits
Cover design: Ian Koo
Interior design & typesetting: Adrian So
Cover image: © Photodisc/Thinkstock
Printer: Printcrafters

John Wiley & Sons Canada, Ltd.
6045 Freemont Blvd.
Mississauga, Ontario
L5R 4J3

Printed in Canada

1 2 3 4 5 PC 15 14 13 12 11

MIX
Paper from
responsible sources
FSC® C003958

ENVIRONMENTAL BENEFITS STATEMENT
Using 9479 lb of Rolland Enviro100 Print instead of virgin fibres paper reduces John Wiley & Sons Canada, Ltd. ecological footprint by:

TREES	SOLID WASTE	WATER	AIR EMISSIONS
81	5,117	48,382	11,237
FULLY GROWN	POUNDS	GALLONS	POUNDS

It's the equivalent of :
Tree(s) : 1.67 american football field(s)
Water : a shower of 10.1 day(s)
Air emissions : emissions of 1.03 car(s) per year

Acknowledgments

Although *Outlaw Biker* is a work of fiction, it would be incorrect to think of it as a one-person effort. I'd like to thank all of my sources who told me stories about life in the places the book talks about, but I'm pretty sure they wouldn't want me to mention their names here. I would also like to thank my wife's friend Gulnara for introducing me to many different cultures from the former Soviet Union; my wife and kids for their patience; the team at Wiley, especially super editor Don Loney; and, of course, Leta Potter, without whom nothing gets done.

Chapter One

It was a surprisingly desolate place considering it was in the middle of a big city. Ned knew that Detroit had fallen on some really hard times, but he was shocked at the utter emptiness of this part of the city, just outside the downtown core. He watched for any sign of human activity. It was as though some kind of epidemic or radiation had devastated the place. He kept the windows rolled up and the doors locked.

There were, of course, lots of reminders that this had once been a very busy place—the empty factories with their broken windows, abandoned cars, piles of trash and boarded-up houses gave mute testimony to that—but there were no people. He thought he saw a stray dog—maybe a coyote—hunting what were probably rats in a pile of trash.

He wondered exactly why his new friends from work—Chuck and Bob—had sent him to this almost post-apocalyptic zone. His instructions were to deliver a package, which he guessed contained cash, to an address the GPS that they had supplied him with said was now less than a quarter-mile away. But he couldn't figure out why anyone would want to be out here and he began to get nervous about the kind of people who would be waiting for him.

He had managed to avoid thinking about it in any kind of depth for the whole trip. But ever since he had left Wilmington almost ten hours ago, he had been nagged by the feeling that he might be in the middle of a setup. How well did he know Chuck and Bob anyway? He had quickly spotted that they were operators. Ned could tell from their cars, clothes and behavior that they were obviously guys with something going on. They were small-time to be sure, but they could easily have some big connections.

And Ned woke up and went to sleep every day knowing that there were more than a few people— maybe those very connections who supplied Chuck and Bob—who very badly wanted to see him dead. Ned's testimony had put a lot of bikers—his former brothers in the Sons of Satan—away, some for a very long time. The FBI was hiding him behind a new identity, but he knew the Sons of Satan and their allies were everywhere, and Ned also knew that moving him from the Midwest to the east coast was no guarantee that someone wouldn't hunt him down.

The FBI guys were pretty smart about it, though. Delaware didn't have any Sons of Satan chapters. In fact, none of the major biker clubs had a clubhouse in the state. But that didn't mean bikers only went there for a bit of R&R.

Traditionally, all of Delaware's organized crime was run by the Philadelphia Mafia. But after the successive failures of Little Nicky Scarfo, Johnny Stanfa and Ralph Natale to keep their men in line and out of prison, their power was waning, especially on the fringes of their empire. By the late 1990s, a sizeable chunk of the drug trade in the tiny state was controlled from a distance by bikers: Pagans from Maryland or Hells Angels from Virginia. There was no love lost between the two clubs, but both had been known to ally with the Sons of Satan depending on which way the winds were prevailing.

Chuck and Bob, the two guys Ned worked with in the mailroom of a credit-assessment agency, could very easily have been paid to deliver him to the Sons of Satan. They had, after all, sent him on a trip here, to the

Midwest. Detroit, Ned knew, was traditionally the heart of Outlaws territory, but he also knew that the Sons of Satan were never very far away.

Sweating, he stopped the car. He didn't pull over; he just threw the car into park. He closed his eyes and put his head in his hands. Ned realized that there was a very strong possibility that he was being sent to his death. He thought about it. Who the hell were Chuck and Bob anyway? He didn't even know their real names. Why should he trust them? All he wanted to do was make a quick buck and break up the boredom of his job. And when these two Serbian guys who worked with him recognized his biker tattoos and offered him a pile of money to deliver a small package, he thought it might be fun.

But then he thought about the odds. If Chuck and Bob knew that the Sons of Satan wanted him dead, they would certainly have made a move by now. And they didn't seem smart or sophisticated enough to pull something like this off. If they wanted to kill him, they wouldn't put him in a car with a GPS and a thick manila envelopé and send him so far across the country; they'd just whack him in the head with a crowbar. He actually couldn't help laughing to himself as he pictured it—Chuck laying on the beating and Bob going through his pockets.

Ned wanted to get the hell out of the neighborhood. Even the plan he'd made to legitimize the trip wasn't relieving his anxiety. If he couldn't trust Chuck and Bob, then he sure as hell couldn't trust the people at the other end. But a life of drudgery was no life. Live free or die.

He quickly looked around. The street was deserted. He picked up the envelope and tore off a strip. Cash. Lots of it. Ned threw the transmission into "drive." A couple of blocks later, he saw exactly where he was headed. The building looked a lot like all the others in the area—low and broad with that bit of ornate flair you don't see in buildings made after a certain era. Unlike the others, it had all of its doors and windows intact. But that's not what made it stand out. While its neighbors were surrounded by trash, piles of tires or abandoned vehicles, the area around this building was cleaned up. The parking lot sported a number of luxury cars and SUVs, all of them modified to some degree and some of them painted in outrageous colors.

Ned parked in an open spot between a bright purple Cadillac SUV and a snow-white Corvette. He got out of the car and noticed that he wasn't alone. A young man who looked big with a shaven head and a mustache sat in a small, late-model BMW with an aftermarket spoiler on the trunk. Ned nodded at him. The man did not acknowledge him; instead, he pulled out a cell phone and started to make a call.

Ned approached the door, which was solid steel, black and windowless. Ned noticed one of those cheap, white, boxy video cameras mounted about ten feet up. It was pointed directly at the space in front of the door. He looked directly at it, smiled and resisted the urge to wave. There was an intercom system beside the door. Ned pressed the "speak" button and said, "Delivery."

Ned heard a long buzz and the lock mechanism activated. He pulled the door open and walked in. Before his eyes could adjust to the darkness inside, someone threw a cloth sack over his head and pulled him to the ground. He was rolled on his stomach and his hands cuffed behind his back. A hand grabbed the collar of his sweatshirt and Ned was pulled roughly to his feet. Orders were barked in a language Ned didn't know and the sack was secured around his neck. One of the men grabbed him by his left bicep and guided him deeper into the building. The men began talking to each other and one kept giggling. Ned identified at least four distinct voices. He heard a door open. The man leading him stepped down. "Careful," a heavily accented voice said to Ned. "Stairs."

Although he knew he was going down the steps, it was hard to negotiate them while blindfolded. Ned took each step cautiously and tenuously, but stumbled twice. Every time he slipped, the laughing guy giggled.

Down the stairs, Ned was guided a few more steps and then roughly pushed down into an armchair. He heard some talking back and forth, then he felt the sack being loosened. As soon as the sack was removed, Ned was momentarily blinded by a light.

When his eyes finally adjusted, he could see he was in a windowless basement. The only source of light was a naked bulb hanging from the ceiling no more than eighteen inches from his face. The cement walls were full of cracks and had black marks and patches of mold or lichen. It smelled dank.

Ned was in a smelly old armchair. Directly in front of him was a massively fat man in an expensive suit. He had a wide face with a downturned, toad-like mouth. He had combed and shellacked his thinning black hair over the top of his bald head and had a wide scar on his right cheek. His smile revealed two gold teeth. As Ned continued to look at him, he saw more and more gold. Rings on just about every finger, bracelets as thick as a man's thumb on each wrist, big cufflinks and at least four thick chains were visible before his shirt closed.

One each side of him were two very big, very hairy men in garishly colored nylon track suits. One had a wife beater on underneath and the other was shirtless.

Every square inch of them except for their heads, necks and hands looked to be covered in ornate tattoos. They both had shaved heads and goatees. Similarly dressed thugs were standing on each side of Ned's chair. Off a few steps was a young, thinner guy who could barely contain his excitement. Ned identified him as the giggler. He turned his head around and saw another man sitting in a chair. Unlike the others, this guy had neither a beer belly nor manufactured muscles. He was small and slim and was wearing a conventional tailored suit. He was the only one who was not awash in gold and emblazoned with tattoos. When Ned caught his eye, the man in the chair nodded emotionlessly. The nod drew attention to the fact that he was holding a rather large handgun.

Ned looked at the smiling fat man in front of him. "Who are you?" the man asked in heavily accented English.

"I'm delivering a package from Chuck and Bob."

"I did not ask you that." The tone was flat and menacing.

Ned could feel the bile rising in his throat. His heart was pounding insistently. If they were more interested in him than the package, it was not a good sign. Realizing that too long a pause would make him look like he was hiding something, he blurted out, "I'm Eric

Steadman." It was the name the FBI had given him when he entered the witness protection program.

"Eric Steadman. Eric Steadman from the mailroom," the fat man said, as though considering the name deeply. "Steadman? That is a German name, no?"

"No," said Ned. "It's English, my ancestors came from England I guess . . ."

"Maybe," said the fat man, who was now pacing and not looking at him.

"He looks Scottish to me," he heard a calm, less-accented voice from the back say. "Maybe Norwegian." That assessment chilled Ned, who was in fact mostly of Scottish origin. Could they know Steadman was not his real name? If they did, it was also likely they knew who he was. Since they spoke in English, he knew he was meant to hear them.

The fat man said something in what Ned now took to be Russian, and one of the thugs beside him went over and lifted Ned to his feet. "Empty your pockets. Everything."

Ned handed over his wallet, keys, cell phone and loose change. The thug passed his wallet to the fat man, who opened it, removed a few cards and dropped the rest on the floor. He examined Ned's driver's license in minute detail. Then his Social Security card. After about two minutes, he smiled and shook his head. Then he said something to his men, who all laughed. "I'm something of an expert in these matters," the fat man said to Ned. "And I have never seen such exquisite forgeries in all my life. They look so close to real that they could have fooled me in other circumstances. Tell me, Mr. Steadman, where did you get these?"

The truth, of course, was that they were real. The FBI had given them to him with his new identity. But he couldn't tell them who he really was. These guys might not be bikers, but they were obviously involved in organized crime. They would not take kindly to an informant who testified against his former gang and had close ties to the FBI.

While he was deliberating, one of the thugs whacked him in the back of the head with a beefy paw. He didn't say anything, but it was clear that he wouldn't be allowed any more time to stall the fat man. Slightly dazed from the blow, Ned answered. "I have a guy, he's from Thailand," he said. "Used to make phone cards for me; then copies of credit cards." There was some truth in that. He did know a guy from Thailand who made fake phone cards and credit cards. The Sons of Satan had made a lot of money with him.

The fat man smiled. "Good. I shall have to meet this master craftsman, this artist," he said. "You will introduce me."

Ned couldn't help sighing with relief. That slight clue that Ned might have a future outside of the room he was in led him to believe that he may just survive this meeting.

The fat man said something in Russian and the thug beside Ned stood him up again. He lifted Ned's sweatshirt and t-shirt over his head and said a single word to the fat man. When he was back in his chair, Ned felt the cold metal of the thin man's gun pressing into the back of his head.

"So, now, there remains a few awkward questions," the fat man told Ned in a scolding voice. "The first, obviously, is who you really are."

Cornered, Ned knew he had to come up with something quick. If these guys had been communicating with Chuck and Bob, they knew he was a biker. They had identified him as one by the tattoo his old boss had made him get. The gun at his head insisted he did not hesitate. Ned blurted out, "My name is Jared Macnair."

He hadn't made it up. There really was a Jared Macnair. Ned had heard that he was a secretary of the Sons of Satan chapter in Yuma, Arizona, until he was caught stealing thirty-five thousand dollars in club funds. With a death sentence on his head, Macnair had gone into hiding. Nobody had seen or heard from him for at least a year.

The fat man grinned wryly. Then he nodded to the man behind Ned. The gun withdrew. The fat man took a cell phone out of his suit's breast pocket. He pressed two keys and waited. Finally, he said, "It's me." Pause. "Give me details on a Jerry Macnair, a biker." He looked at Ned during the long pause. Ned did not correct him. "Yes, okay, okay, okay . . . good . . . what does he look like?" The fat man nodded as he listened, and looked intently at Ned. "Yes, yes, blue eyes, dark hair, what? What is six-foot-two?" One of the thugs said something in Russian. Ned could make out something that sounded like "centimeter." The fat man sized Ned up and asked the person he called about tattoos. Ned's entire body clenched. "Okay, okay, yes, yes, it's good, thank you." Then he hung up. He said something to the grizzly bear-shaped man beside Ned. The man then took the handcuffs off. Ned had bet right. He knew they'd kill a rat, but they had no beef with an embezzler.

The fat man offered his hand. "A pleasure to meet you, Macnair," he said with a wide, satisfied grin. "I am Grigori." Ned smiled weakly and shook his hand. The other men in the room laughed. "But I have more questions . . . why is my package open?"

Ned stammered. "I don't know Chuck and Bob that well . . . and I have some enemies . . ."

"Yes, I would say that you do."

". . . and I wanted to make sure I was carrying . . ."

"Money."

"Yes, money. When I saw that it was money in the package, I realized it that it had to be a legitimate delivery."

Grigori said something to the giggler, who Ned noticed had the envelope in his hands. He answered back quickly. Grigori laughed. "So this man, this Macnair, will steal lots of money from his brothers in Sons of Satan gang, but will not steal a penny from me," he said. "He is very smart."

Everyone in the room laughed, and Ned did his best to join in.

Grigori said something in Russian, and the big man put his wallet back in order and handed it to him, along with his cell phone, keys and cash. Grigori barked out something else and the brutish young man handed Ned fifteen hundred dollars. "Okay, Macnair, you have done your job; you go back now to those two Serbian idiots and tell them to be more careful next time," Grigori said with what seemed like sincere warmth. "And if you are asked to make this trip again, the package is never opened . . . you got that?"

"I got that," Ned's voice cracked halfway through the sentence. The men in the room laughed.

"Here, Semyon will show you out."

Semyon, the man Ned identified as the giggler, approached him and shook his hand. "This way," he said, motioning over his right shoulder.

As they walked up the stairs together, Ned could hear the men in the basement talking and laughing. He looked at Semyon. He was maybe in his late twenties, thin and full of energy. Unlike the other guys in track suits, he had not shaved his head and his face was clean-shaven. He had a few tattoos and the same fondness for gold that the other men had, but clearly had not collected nearly as much. He was smiling at Ned, which made him think Semyon expected him to say something.

"Is this how you guys treat everybody who shows up at your door?" he asked.

Semyon cackled like a chimpanzee. "You can't be too careful," he said. "We did not know you, you could be anyone . . . the Serbians . . . they are, like Grigori says, idiots. They could have sent DEA or even FBI without knowing it."

Ned acknowledged his statement with a snort.

Semyon continued. "The Serbians thought you were a cop spying on them at first. Why else would a white American who is not stupid work in a mailroom?" He laughed again. "They told Grigori about you, he told them how to spot if you are cop or not, they saw your tattoo, told him about it, then he said he wanted to meet you."

"And this is how he meets people?"

"Some, if he thinks he might want to work with them."

"Oh, so I have a future with this company?"

"You're alive, aren't you?"

Chapter Two

Ned sat in the driver's seat of the Kia. He drew his hands over his hair a couple of times nervously, sighed and gave into an involuntary shudder. He remembered the man in the BMW. He turned to see if the car was occupied. Ned's eyes locked with his watcher's. Ned turned the key and felt a little bit calmer when he heard the engine spring to life. He pulled out of the parking lot and back onto the road. He felt like taking a different way back, but the whole area looked equally depressing and there was a strong chance he could accidentally wander into an even less pleasant neighborhood.

His thoughts flashed back to what had just happened. He had been afraid for his life, had had a gun pointed at the back of his brain, but somehow he felt good about the whole thing. Not only was fifteen hundred bucks a decent amount of money for a weekend car trip, but the fact that he had fooled the Russians gave him a shot of confidence he had not had since he had decided to turn informant. Maybe he wasn't going to spend the rest of his life in the mailroom after all.

He was thinking about how he could quit his job without Dave Hiltz, his FBI caseworker, going nuts, when he saw a car coming up fast behind him. At first it was maybe a half-mile away, but now it filled up his rearview mirror. It was so close behind that Ned could no longer see its headlights.

It looked like a low-rent gangster's car. It was a Mercedes C-class, maybe ten years old. It was painted a sort of burned-looking brown and all the chrome trim was gold-plated. The windows (even the windshield) were blacked-in, so Ned could not make out the driver's face, or even if there was more than one person in the car.

Ned knew he couldn't outrun his pursuer, but he had to try to get to a more populated area. He floored the Kia. With a reluctant and wheezy whoosh, the Kia took off. Ned was not surprised to see the Mercedes make up lost ground right away. Just as Ned passed through an intersection, he saw something that surprised him.

Through the windshield of the Mercedes, he could see a flashing red light. As soon as he noticed it, he heard the siren.

Ned wasn't sure if it was a real cop or not. It certainly didn't look like a cop car, but he knew that cops used cars seized from drug dealers as camouflage. He pulled to the side of the road. The Mercedes pulled in behind him.

"Driver, please put your hands on the back of your head and exit the vehicle," a loudspeaker-assisted voice ordered. Ned complied. "Keep facing forward!" the voice commanded.

Ned didn't look back. He heard the car door open and close and the steps of the officer as he approached him. "Do you know why I stopped you?"

"I went through a stop sign."

"That's part of it."

Ned didn't know what to say. He remained silent.

"Yeah, uh-huh, what's a nice boy like you doin' here?" The plainclothes cop made a sweeping gesture, as if to introduce Ned to the neighborhood.

"Just passing through."

"Just passing though, eh? The problem with that, you see, is that I saw your car parked for almost an hour among all those Cadillacs and Lexuses over there."

"I was asking directions."

"Funny man," the cop said. "This could have been so easy, but you just had to screw me around." He placed a handcuff on one wrist and then the other. "Siddown here," he said, dumping Ned on the curb. He was a big man, about forty-five years old with a bowling-pin physique in a cheap gray suit and a small, almost childish head. His skin was very dark and his hair extremely short. When he talked, Ned could see he had a big space between his two front teeth. "You mind if I search your car?"

Ned knew there wasn't anything incriminating in the Kia, but he didn't want to make it easier for the cop either. "I do mind."

"Well, then, I'm just gonna have to impound it," the cop said to him. "Uh-huh, gonna call a tow truck, have your shitbox taken to the pound, all at your expense, uh-huh. What do you say to that, funny man? Probably run you maybe eight hundred bucks."

"Okay, okay, search the car."

"Naw, don't feel like it anymore," he said. "How about you just tell me what you were doing in that building and I'll see if I can just write you up a ticket?"

"All you got me for is going through a stop sign."

"And wreckless driving and obstruction of official procedure—and if I think that's pot I smell on you, you could be in a whole lot more trouble, uh huh."

"You haven't even read me my rights yet."

"I'm pretty sure you've heard 'em before," the cop said, leading him over to the Mercedes. "C'mon, into the car, we're going in."

The cop showed him his badge and introduced himself as Detective Halliday, and asked Ned again what he was doing in the neighborhood, and why he had been in the building for almost an hour.

Ned smiled and stalled. He knew his Delaware plates made it unlikely that he would have just stumbled into this neighborhood. He planned on needing a story for moments like these. No point being a stranger in a strange land without a story. With the money the FBI had given him when he turned state's witness, he had bought himself a 1956 Indian motorcycle as something of a reward. He'd found getting his much-needed replacement parts to be tough (the motorcycle was more than fifty years old, after all). There was a dealer in Detroit and he realized he could tell the cops—or anyone else he'd need to convince—that he was looking for the dealer's shop.

Ned explained that he was there looking for parts. "They advertised on Craigslist that they had parts, and they're really rare," he said. "But this represents a major investment for me, so I had to check them out before I bought anything."

"And?"

"And they have some good stuff there, it's definitely Indian and from the era," he said. "But nothing I need right away."

The cop looked him up and down, obviously sizing him up and assessing him for signs of nervousness. "What if I told you those parts are probably stolen?"

Ned grinned. "I'd say I was surprised."

"Yeah? Why's that?"

"Aren't stolen goods usually sold cheap?"

The cop snorted out a small laugh. "You come to a part of town that looks like this to a building that is not only not crumbling from disrepair but attracts an affluent clientele, and you don't even smell a rat? Listen, son, do yourself a big favor and stay away from here."

"I will, I will. So I'm free to go?"

"Just as soon as I finish writing up your ticket . . . you don't think you can run stop signs and get away with it, do you? Things can't be that different in Delaware."

Ned sighed. "No, sir, they are not."

He took his ticket from Halliday and waited to be let out of the car. As he stood up, he caught the cop's eye again. "Seriously, I see your stupid face or your piece-of-shit car in this neighborhood again, I'll throw your ass in jail and then take my time figuring out what's going on with you."

"I understand," Ned said as he walked back to his car. After he got in, he made a big deal out of putting on his seatbelt, looking both ways and signaling as he took off. He saw Halliday get back in his car and turn the opposite way, back towards the clubhouse.

Ned took a right as the GPS instructed, and had barely straightened out when he heard his phone ring insistently. He looked at it. The display flashed "Unknown caller." He answered.

Even before he could say hello, he heard a heavily accented voice ask, "What did you tell him?"

"What did I tell who? Who is this?"

"What did you tell the cop?"

Realizing that stalling wasn't going to help him, Ned replied, "Nothing."

"I'm serious, Macnair. What exactly did you tell him?"

Ned pulled over. "I told him the truth—that I was lost in this big city and stopped to ask for directions." He heard the man on the other side laugh, then continued. "I also told him they invited me in for a drink. Since I have no criminal record, he let me go with a ticket."

"Give the ticket to the Serbians, they will take care of it."

Then the man hung up.

Chapter Three

Even before he arrived at work Monday morning, Ned
had even more contempt for his dead-end job. His taste
of adventure and money making had made him hungry
for more. And it had ratcheted up his dislike for his job
and the people there. When Dolores—a short, fat and
smug woman who liked to laugh at things that weren't
funny and had decorated her cubicle with hundreds of
photos of her cats—told him that he looked like he had
"a bad case of the Mondays," it was all he could do not
to smack her.

Chuck and Bob had been avoiding him. When Ned
finally cornered Chuck, all the Serbian would say was
"wait until lunch."

When lunch break finally arrived, Ned was anxious. Chuck and Bob ushered him outside. The few picnic tables on the grassy area beside the building were already filling up with chattering employees. In good weather Ned and the Serbians usually ate in the parking lot with the Mexicans, but they passed by their normal spot without stopping. Instead, they took him to a freeway on-ramp about a hundred yards away. It was so loud beside the steady stream of cars that they literally had to shout to hear one another.

"They like you!" Chuck told him. "They want you to come back! They think you are funny."

Ned smiled. "I don't know about that. I got stopped by a detective on the way back. I think he's watching who goes in and out pretty good."

"Don't worry about cops," Bob said.

"No, this guy seemed pretty adamant."

"What is 'adamant'?"

"Serious, he was serious."

"Only because cops have no sense of humor."

"No, this one knows what's going on."

"Really? I don't even know what's going on," said Chuck. Then he paused. "Look, if you don't want to work for us, that's fine we can always . . ."

"I didn't say that," Ned said, hoping he hadn't sounded too desperate. "It's just that this cop . . ."

"Let us take care of the cops."

Ned felt his phone vibrate. He pulled it out of his pocket. The call display indicated that he was getting a call from "Asshole." He pointed to it. "I gotta take this," he told Chuck and Bob and started walking away from the on-ramp.

When it was quiet enough, he answered. "Hey, Dave, waddaya want?"

"Hey now, is that any way to talk to the man who keeps you alive and out of prison?" Dave asked mockingly. "How about a 'How was your weekend?' or 'How's it going?'"

Ned grunted.

"Okay, be that way," Dave said. "But you have got some pretty big questions to answer, my young friend."

"Like what?"

"Like what the fuck you were doing in the middle of Detroit without telling me?"

"Well, I . . ."

"Stop right there, I don't have time for one of your bullshit stories right now. Get your ass in here tomorrow."

"I got work."

"I'll call your boss. Just get in here. If we make it three, you can have the rest of the afternoon off without you having to go back to work."

"Thanks."

"Whatever, but you had better have a good reason and you had better be telling the truth. If it's anything other than someone stole your car and your wallet and drove to the Motor City, you could find yourself in a world of shit."

"I understand. Tomorrow at three then."

Chuck and Bob had gone back to the parking lot to eat. Ned joined them, and they talked about lots of things, none of which had anything to do with what happened in Detroit.

As one o'clock approached, people began filing back into the building at different rates. Ned trudged back in between Chuck and Bob. "I don't see how it's going to work out," he told them.

"Don't worry about the details," Chuck said. "We will work it out."

* * *

Ned did not actively hate Dave—and he knew that his association with the FBI had allowed him not only to beat a murder rap, but had also probably saved his life—but there were few things he hated more than visiting his watchdog. Sometimes they met at coffee shops or fast-food places, but when they had something serious to talk about, they met at his office.

Since a big part of Dave's job involved meeting with victims, witnesses and those in the witness protection program, he had a small office in Marcus Hook, Pennsylvania, about halfway between Wilmington and the FBI's regional headquarters in Philadelphia. It was upstairs from an old knick-knack shop and had a sign that read "F & E Schwartz, Immigration Law." Ned asked him about it once and Dave said it kept locals from nosing around and "justified the clientele."

Inside, it was a stuffy, nearly windowless office cluttered with the sorts of detritus an immigration lawyer might require. Dave was behind the desk. He was a robust, red-faced man with what had once been reddish blond hair. His ruddy complexion was made worse by his habit of wearing blue shirts with white collars and cuffs and augmenting them with gold pins and cufflinks. Nearly always a size or two too small and crisply starched, his shirts seemed to be struggling to hold in his saggy neck. He turned to face Ned when he heard him enter, and Ned saw that his watery blue eyes were looking at him with a great deal of suspicion.

"How's my favorite snitch?"

Ned just smirked. "Hey Dave."

"You have a lot of explaining to do, little mister."

"Do I?"

"I'd say so . . . hmm, ah, here it is . . . I get to work

on Monday morning and get this." He tossed a printout of a spreadsheet to Ned, who was now seated across the desk from him. Ned could see the name "Eric Steadman" covered in neon pink highlighter. Beside it was a charge and farther along was the place of the infraction and some other factual information, including the name "Det. Halliday." Dave snorted, and asked "What do you have to say to that, Sonny Jim?"

Ned smiled as confidently as he could muster and shook his head. "I got a ticket."

Dave looked as him with a face that was half condescending and half beseeching. "While I realize that running a stop sign isn't really a federal matter," he said to Ned mockingly, "the fact that you drove about six hundred miles through—wait, Delaware, Jersey? No, not Jersey. Pennsylvania, Ohio and Michigan—four states just to get one is actually what I find interesting."

Remembering that his "looking for parts" story worked well with the cop in Detroit, he tried it again. "Y'know my bike?"

"Yeah, I know your bike," Dave scoffed. "The one I told you not to buy because it makes you stand out? The one that makes you easily recognized and therefore vulnerable? The one I told you repeatedly not to buy? Yeah, I remember that bike."

"Well, it needs parts."

"Of course it does," Dave hissed. "The damn thing's older than Jesus."

"Yeah, and these guys have them," Ned softened his tone, feigning contrition. "I knew you were against the bike in the first place and would be angry if I went cross-country for parts, so I didn't want to tell you."

Ned looked at him questioningly.

"And not telling me could lead to the end of your eligibility for the program and perhaps even criminal charges and potentially prison time."

Ned's look of anxiety was genuine.

"Yeah, there are a lot of guys inside and out who'd like nothing better than to be known as the guy who killed off Ned Aiken," Dave said gravely. "You lose our support, and you might as well put a 'shoot me' sign on your back." He couldn't help but laugh a little.

Ned sighed and said, "Understood."

* * *

Ned had hardly gotten back to his place when he slumped down in the only chair in his one-room apartment. He really wanted to lie down in bed, but that would be too much like giving up. He took the Wendy's burger and fries he had bought himself for dinner out of the paper bag, and absent-mindedly turned on the TV. As he was unwrapping his dinner, his phone rang. "Unknown number" flashed on the display. Ned thought about ignoring it, but eventually answered. "Hello."

"Eric, it's me, Chuck," said the voice on the other side. "You eaten dinner yet?"

"I was just about to."

"Look, we wanted to talk with you after work but when you left early we did not have a chance," Chuck said. "We have a few important things to discuss—things that will make you very happy."

Ned laughed. "I'm kinda busy right now."

"No, you aren't."

Ned laughed for real this time. "Okay, you got me, you can buy me dinner."

"Good, go to the Sandwich Shoppe out in Hilltop."

Ned knew where it was. He didn't live far away. "Right. Well, it's better than what I have. What time?"

"We're already here."

* * *

It did not take Ned long to get there. It looked like any one of the thousands of Sandwich Shoppes across the States, except this one had a "Closed" sign on the door. Ned found that to be strange considering that it was probably the busiest time of day for such a restaurant, except maybe for lunch. He saw Bob and Chuck inside and tried the door. It was locked. Chuck saw him, walked over and unlocked the door.

"Hey, Eric. Come on in." Ned noticed he locked the door behind him.

"Shouldn't this place be open?" he asked. "There's nothing wrong with the food, is there?"

"No, no, no, no, food is fine," laughed Chuck. "The owner is good friend of mine, lets me use restaurant as meeting place when is necessary."

"Won't he lose business?"

"Entire neighborhood is nothing but Mexicans and other new immigrants—the thought of Italian sand-wiches confuses them, they don't eat here," Chuck said. "Besides, I pay him." Then he shouted something in Serbian and the guy behind the counter nodded with what appeared to be a great deal of resignation. "Back home, I used to work for him," Chuck said, pointing over his shoulder at the dark and haggardly older man. "He was a mean boss—what you call asshole here, but we have worse name back home—now he works for me, and he finds I am maybe even meaner boss." He shouted something at the man who was hurriedly making sand-wiches. Ned wasn't sure what the man said back, but he appeared to be trying to get Chuck to calm down or at least get off his back. He brought the three of them sandwiches and retreated behind the counter where he sat in a chair and read a newspaper. No matter what Chuck said about paying him, Ned could tell this guy was some pissed off at missing his dinner rush.

"Can we talk in front of him?" Ned pointed at the old man.

Chuck laughed. "Oh yeah, his English is not too good and I own him anyway." Bob laughed too. The old guy looked up then went back to his reading.

Bob spoke first. "They like you, man. They want you to work for them."

"I told you, it's not gonna happen."

"I forgot, you love the mailroom too much."

"No, there was a cop there; he arrested me, he warned me, he knows my face."

"A city cop? You are worried about this?" Chuck muttered something in Serbian to Bob. They both laughed. "I heard bikers were pussies, but now I know." They laughed again. "A city cop we can take care of. It's not like it's the FBI."

Ned hoped they didn't see the minute flinch he succumbed to when they mentioned the FBI. "Wait, why am I so important that they'd hit a cop for me?"

"Don't worry, they won't hurt your boyfriend," Bob laughed. "But they do want you."

"Well, the real problem for me isn't the cop, it's the location. Detroit is crawling with bikers."

"Suppose the business they wanted you to get involved with is not in Detroit or even Midwest?"

Ned was intrigued. "What is it?"

"That will become clear in time."

"Okay, so why me?"

"That should be obvious; you do not look like a criminal, you look like young businessman—at least if we clean you up. You can go places, do things without arousing suspicion. It's almost like police can't see you, you are invisible to them."

"But why me? Why not some other white guy?"

"Because you *are* a criminal, you have tasted the life and want some more . . . or maybe you want forty more years in the mailroom."

Ned contemplated for a moment. "Okay, there are complications . . ."

"There always are," said Chuck, who was appeared to be in charge of the pair. "What do you want?"

"I'll need a whole pack of ID, good stuff, enough to get past a cop or over the border."

"Is not a problem. What name?"

"My real name—Jared Macnair."

Chapter Four

The guy beside Ned stank. Not just a little, but a real, hardcore days-and-days-of-sweat-and-urine stink. That didn't bother him as much as the incessant scratching. But he didn't have much choice. Ned couldn't afford his own computer, let alone an internet account, so he used the public computers at the local library at least once a week. He avoided the computers in the children's department, dominated by screaming kids playing online games of the shoot-to-kill variety.

He used his free twenty-minute session to catch up on news of the Sons of Satan trial. His testimony had gone into the record long ago, but it was a complicated set of trials and the sheer number of defendants demanded that the process took a long time. And the savvier defense attorneys did their best to prolong it so that witnesses began to question their own memories or grow more reluctant to testify for other reasons.

Ned knew that his testimony was going to send Bouchard and Mehelnechuk—the leaders of the Sons of Satan—away for a long time. But he was surprised just how many members of the gang were already set free—or about to be—through shrewd plea bargaining or due to missing or incomplete evidence. In fact, most of the gang was out of custody and, he knew, likely to be re-forming even as he was reading about them.

Normally, he just looked at the names and faces and put them in a mental database—more, he convinced himself, for nostalgia than out of fear that the Sons of Satan would attempt to hunt him down and kill him. But then he saw a name that evoked in him an emotion he had not felt about the trial until that moment.

The name was Dario Gagliano. Dario had been the closest thing Ned had to a real friend in the Sons of Satan, but he was also the reason he turned informant. Ned still vividly recalled the altercation in which he unintentionally killed an innocent man, and Dario had helped him get rid of the body. After they were all arrested in a massive police operation, Ned realized that everyone who knew he had killed someone were all either dead or had more to lose by talking than he did. Except for Dario. Ned had run into him—drug-addled and looking like he was about to crack—when the police were interrogating them all. And he panicked. Ned knew that he could plea bargain his way into a short, tolerable prison stay if all they had on him was trafficking and conspiracy, but if Dario had sold him out or even let slip that he'd killed someone, dismembered and hidden the corpse, Ned knew he was looking at twenty years or even more. So he made a quick decision: Turn state's evidence, and sell everyone else out for a get-out-of-jail-free card.

And he was right. Dario did turn informant, no more than a half hour after he did. Even though his life in the witness protection program was pretty shitty, Ned often told himself, it beat twenty in supermax.

At least that's what he told himself, until today. According to *The Springfield Silhouette*, Dario's testimony had been declared inadmissible due to his "advanced psychosis and deteriorating mental capacity brought on by years of heavy stimulant drug use."

Ned realized that if he had been a good soldier and kept his mouth shut like he had been taught that he'd probably have been out by now.

He remembered what happened when a member of the Sons of Satan returned from jail or prison. There would be a party in his honor, and anything he wanted—booze, drugs, strippers, prostitutes—was taken care of. And if he'd stayed quiet and out of trouble behind bars, there would often be a reward or a promotion for him.

But there would be no party for Ned or Eric or Jared or whatever name he was going by these days. Just another night of boredom, as it had been since they had brought him here.

The FBI hadn't exactly lied to him, but they weren't exactly on the up and up with him either. They did give him a house and a job and twenty thousand in cash like they said they would. But they moved him out of the house when a family of four from Nevada needed it (after all, he was a single man, why did he need that much space?), the job was the shittiest one in the world (but what could he, a high school dropout with nothing but drug sales on his résumé, expect?) and the twenty thousand was quickly eaten up when he had to replace pretty much everything he owned and buy that gift for himself—the Indian. As it stood, he had a dark, cramped apartment, a humiliating minimum-wage job, no friends, no girl and not much hope for a better future.

He called Chuck. "Yeah man, I'm ready to talk with your buddy."

"It's already done."

"What do you mean?"

"We need to talk in person," Chuck said. "Go to the sandwich place in Hilltop."

* * *

Just as he was getting out of the Kia in front of the restaurant, Ned heard the low, loud rumble of a customized Harley-Davidson. Reflexively, he jumped back into the car, and ducked down. Once it was clear the Harley had gone by, he sat up and looked around. There was a round-faced kid—maybe eight years old—looking at him through the passenger window. At first the kid looked mystified, and then he started to laugh before running away.

Ned couldn't laugh at himself as he tried to regain his dignity. The nearest Son of Satan was a thousand miles away; that Harley was probably some rich old dude trying to look cool. Though why that kind of guy would be driving down the worst block in the poorest neighborhood of town raised a little doubt in Ned's mind.

The restaurant was doing a comparatively brisk business. Chuck and Bob were in the back at a table. They looked different than they did at work. Instead of minor clues as to their wealth, like expensive watches, they were in full gangster wear with expensive shell suits and loads of gold. After sitting down and exchanging greetings, Ned asked why they had to meet in a public place, especially this one.

"We have nothing to say that is at all con-tro-ver-sial," Bob said. Ned could tell Bob enjoyed using the word "controversial."

"So what are we here to talk about?"

Chuck yelled something at shop's owner, who nodded with resignation. "Our mutual friend in the Midwest," he said. "He thinks he likes you, may have some part-time work for you."

"What kind of work?"

"Nothing much, shipping and receiving, that sort of thing, no problem for you."

"Where would it be?"

"Wherever you want—here in Wilmington, maybe—but with a few trips to nearby places like New Jersey and maybe New York City."

"Sounds okay."

"Okay? It's a great opportunity!"

Ned tried hard to look unimpressed. "Maybe it is, but I need to know more."

"Come into the back with me."

As they got up and went behind the counter, Ned noticed Chuck was carrying a yellow envelope. He led

Ned into a small room full of boxes and cleaning supplies. "Grigori has given you two gifts. Here, open this."

Ned opened the envelope. Inside were a passport and a Minnesota driver's license with his likeness on them. They were made out in the name of "Jared Macnair."

Ned looked up at Chuck who was obviously proud. "Remember I took your pictures for security cards at work? I sent them to Grigori who has good friend in passport department," he said excitedly. And another in DMV in Minnesota." He laughed a little at Ned's reaction. "And look, Macnair is spelled right, not McNair like many others," he was practically gushing now. "And has correct birthdate and even hometown of Gila Bend, Arizona."

Realizing it could be a test, Ned corrected Chuck's pronunciation from "GUY-lah" to "HEE-lah."

Chuck laughed. "English is the most strange language," he said. "Do you want your other gift?"

"Isn't this it?"

Chuck smiled broadly. "Do you remember the cop who was bothering you?"

"Yeah, Halliday?" Ned replied. "They didn't . . . "

"No, no, no, no harm will come to your boyfriend," Chuck laughed. "No, but he did come across some very bad luck."

"What happened?" Ned felt his throat dry up.

Chuck laughed again, but this time with less joy. "It seems a young boy, a young Russian boy, has accused the detective of—how do you say it?—molesting him," he said. "Sad, very sad."

"What? Really?"

"Well, nobody can say what happened for sure. But the investigation will, of course, take a long time, and your friend naturally will be suspended—maybe also for a long time."

Ned paused. "I don't know what to say."

"Say thank you."

"Uh—thank you, and thank Grigori."

"He is always good to his employees," said Chuck. Then he sighed and said, "There is one little, tiny thing, though."

Ned felt eerily cold. "What's that?"

Chuck laughed, then grinned. "Nothing, nothing." He paused, then shrugged. "All you have to do is prove you are who and what you say you are—simple."

Ned hoped that Chuck couldn't hear the terror in his voice. "H-how would I do that?"

"Is nothing, really," Chuck's smile had left his face. "You know the Lawbreakers?"

"Yeah."

"They have small chapter in Ocean Beach," Chuck said. "They—and you—have a job to do."

"Lawbreakers? But I'm . . ."

"You're what?"

"Well, I used to be a Sons of Satan full-patch . . ."

"And now you are man who stole from Sons of Satan, got away with it, lived and now works for Grigori, most powerful man in all Midwest."

"If he is so powerful, why does he need me?"

Chuck's face hardened. "He doesn't *need* you. Don't question him. This is just part of your job. You want him to trust you, right? Do what is asked of you."

"Right, but I'm supposed to collaborate with the Lawbreakers? You want me to just walk in blindly to some situation?"

Chuck laughed. "You Americans, always with the worry, worry, worry. No, Grigori would never ask you to do something so stupid. The Ocean Beach Lawbreakers have a bar, you go there and they will welcome you. Remember, you fucked over the Sons of Satan, that makes you a hero in their eyes—and you can bring Semyon, he will help."

Ned knew he didn't have long to decide, and he knew the safest way out of the room he was in would be to agree to do what they asked. If he later decided he couldn't do it, he could always tell Dave and see if the

FBI could move him again. But then, of course, he'd have two sets of criminals who'd want to kill him and probably an even worse job. At least in Delaware he wasn't that far from the beach. Then he remembered that Semyon was the giggler and he let out a little laugh.

Chuck grinned. Ned took that to mean that Chuck was confident that he would go through with it. "Sure, sure, I'll go see these guys," he said, even though he still wasn't sure if he would.

"Good, good," said Chuck. "Semyon will pick you up at your apartment Saturday morning."

"What time?"

"When he gets there," Chuck replied a little harshly, then followed it up with a hearty laugh. "So, you want some sandwich?" He smiled broadly and led Ned back into the restaurant. Bob nodded and grinned when he saw them coming out.

* * *

Since they had started seeing each other outside the mailroom, Ned barely communicated with Chuck and Bob when they were at work. They initiated the little moratorium on contact, and he was more than okay with it. He started eating his lunches alone, and had found that he tended to find reading in the sunshine much more pleasurable than engaging in their inane banter that rarely wavered from women and cars. And he certainly didn't like it when they would start talking to each other in Serbian, invariably ending up laughing at what Ned suspected was him.

By the time Friday rolled around, Ned was happy to put work behind him, but apprehensive about his weekend task and less than delighted to see Dave that evening.

As soon as he got to Dave's office, he started asking him the familiar questions he had asked him every two weeks since Ned had been in the witness protection program. He gave the same answers he always did in what he thought was the same way he always did until Dave interrupted him. "You sound bored, Mr. Steadman; bored with your lot in life," he said in the almost-friendly way he had. "Maybe you're planning another road trip?"

Ned looked at him stunned. He hoped that Dave would interpret his surprise as him thinking the idea preposterous, not that he had read his mind. Ned laughed. "No, not looking to travel," he said with a chuckle. "Looking for some of the other things young men enjoy."

Dave sucked in a deep breath and sighed dramatically. Ned had suspected that Dave might be gay. But now, for the first time, he realized that his minder was also pretty attracted to him. "Hmmm, Ned, I have not for-gotten what it was like to be young myself, you know," he said, looking him in the eye. "Why can't you find yourself a nice girl? It is girls you like, right?"

Ned smiled generously. "Yeah."

"You're a nice-looking, athletic boy; you should have no problem meeting girls," Dave continued. "A nice girl should be able to get past the whole mailroom thing."

Ned was desperate to change the subject. "So I can't travel at all?"

"Not without my permission."

"Even in-state? This tiny, tiny little state?"

"Well, I guess you can't get into too much trouble in Delaware. I'll look the other way in-state."

"Philly?"

"No."

"Jersey?"

"Heavens no! What kind of girl are you looking for anyway?"

Ned laughed. "Just checking. How about Ocean Beach?"

"What's the matter with Reheboth?"

"Too many Jersey boys."

Dave laughed and said, "You've got me there." But then his face turned serious, even cold. "Listen, I know you were some kind of high flier back in the Midwest," he said, trying to sound intimidating. "But now you are a mailroom clerk for a credit-assessment agency in Delaware, you got that?"

Ned tried not to laugh while he nodded.

"You may not be impressed by this office or my wardrobe or my car, but I represent the FBI around here, and we own you," Dave snarled. "And bear in mind, young man, that if I get a hint of any criminal activity—or even if just don't like you—I can get a court order removing your protection. You'd get your old identity back and I could even get them to force you to pay back the money we fronted you. Then where would you be? I'll tell you. You would be broke, alone and sitting in plain sight with a big fat price on your head. How's that grab you?"

Ned tried to look grave. Of course, he had already run the odds in his head, and Dave's posturing struck him as silly and impotent. Ned couldn't think of anything to say but "I'll stay here."

Dave smiled and apologized. "Don't make me order a tracking bracelet."

Ned knew only a judge could do that, but he chuckled amiably and said he wouldn't make any trouble.

* * *

Ned woke up early on Saturday morning because he had no idea when Semyon was going to arrive. He didn't know what to do with himself. He'd read everything in his apartment, he didn't get enough TV channels to watch anything interesting, so he just put on a little music and puttered around his little place, alternatively cleaning, snacking and pacing around.

At around ten, Ned was washing his breakfast dishes when he heard a blast of music that shook his innards. He ran out into the street to see where the noise was coming from. In front of the building, he saw a bright green car—a ten-year-old Lexus with ridiculous spinning rims and gold trim—with all four windows open. The booming bass and high-pitched tweets of Euro house music were pouring out of it, and the whole car was shaking with every beat. Ned approached it cautiously. As he got close enough to touch the car, Semyon popped his head out of his window, grinned goofily and yelled, "Hey, Macnair. Get in."

Ned couldn't help but roll his eyes. He got closer to Semyon, but found he still had to shout to be heard over his gut-busting stereo. "I'll be back in a second. I just gotta lock up," he said to him. "But I'm not getting in that car until you turn that shit off." Semyon laughed and nodded his head.

By the time Ned returned, Semyon had indeed turned his music off. "You really know how to be subtle," Ned said as he got into the passenger seat.

"What is this word 'subtle'?"

"Never mind, it would take a long time to explain and I don't think you would understand even if I did," Ned told him.

Then he paused. "Are we really going to do this, just show up and demand Grigori's friend's money from a bunch of Lawbreakers?"

"Sure, man, sure," Semyon assured him. "It's simple, they owe us, we go pick it up. It's no problem, man." Then he giggled his little giggle.

"Two guys, unarmed."

"Who says unarmed?"

"Well, I am."

"No you're not, man; I have at least a dozen guns in the car, you have your pick—but we won't need them."

"We won't?"

"We won't."

"You're absolutely sure of this?"

Semyon just giggled.

Ned took a moment to size up his new associate. Semyon didn't look like the other Russians he had met. He had darker skin, darker eyes and seemed a bit thicker haired. He looked more like Abdullah, the Palestinian guy he knew from the fast-food place he often bought dinner from, than the other Russians. He had a strange pop-eyed look that made him seem younger than he almost certainly was and his body never stopped moving. It was like every inch of him was nervous all the time.

Ned and Semyon engaged in small talk for most of the two-hour trip. Ned really didn't want to hear any more of Semyon's music, so he kept him talking. It was pretty easy, as Semyon really liked to talk, mostly about himself. He told Ned that he was not actually Russian at all, but an Uzbek. Ned didn't know what an Uzbek was, so Semyon explained that his ancestors came from a Central Asian country called Uzbekistan that had once been ruled by the Russians as part of the Soviet Union.

"Isn't that like where Borat lives?" Ned asked.

Semyon laughed. "That's Kazakhstan—just north of Uzbekistan—they are assholes."

Ned laughed. "So, what is Uzbekistan like?"

"I don't really know," Semyon told him. "I've never been there." He went on to explain that he was born and raised in a south Moscow neighborhood that was mostly Uzbek with a few other nationalities that didn't really register with Ned's consciousness. Semyon's grandfather had been a cotton farmer back in Uzbekistan before he was pressed into the Red Army. Apparently, the old man had quite a talent for machinery, so the Russians allowed him to move to Moscow and work as a truck mechanic. The family had been there ever since. "Just in time, too," Semyon added. "The Muslims have since taken over and made Uzbekistan an even worse place."

Because of the "-stan" in his native country's name, Ned just assumed Semyon was a Muslim. "So how did you get over here?"

"Back in the nineties," he told him, "America was letting in lots of lots of people from the former Soviet Union, mostly skilled workers. One was an Uzbek called Djamolidine who worked in pharmaceuticals. My family raised enough money to convince him to say he is my father's brother. I got a Green Card."

"It was that easy?"

"Back then, yes. But after 9/11 it became much more expensive, and the wait is much longer."

Ned rolled his eyes. Semyon continued to prattle on and on about Uzbeks, Kazakhs, Russians, Moscow, Detroit and what made them all interesting to him. Ned was glad that Semyon was so content to hear himself speak, because keeping up the pretense of being Jared Macnair pretending to be Eric Steadman was taxing enough without having to come up with a detailed back story.

The tourist season hadn't really revved up in Ocean Beach yet, but most of the roadside shops and restaurants were already open when they arrived. Semyon said how much he liked the place, how it reminded him of a resort his family once took him to on the Black Sea when he was a boy and even took some time out to follow two school-age girls until they noticed him and ran down a side street.

They arrived at an old whitewashed and windblown building that had a sign outside that said "Mickey's." There were a couple of customized Harleys out front, a pickup with a Harley-Davidson bumper sticker and a couple of old and beat-up cars. As soon as they got out of Semyon's car, Ned could hear some activity in the area. When he entered the bar, he was surprised at how dim it was inside and was overwhelmed by the odors of stale beer and old fryer grease. There was a bartender doing a crossword puzzle behind the bar. Unbidden, he told Ned and Semyon, "They're out back," and pointed to a door through which Ned could see sunlight pouring in and could hear muffled talking and laughing.

As unwelcoming as the bar itself was, Mickey's wooden beachside patio was quite nice, and it was being enjoyed by about a half-dozen rough-looking men of various ages and a couple of women, who appeared to be in their forties. Ned recognized them as Lawbreakers right away from their clothes, jewelry and tattoos. One even had a picture of "Oscar," the gang's cartoon convict mascot, tattooed on his neck.

The patio fell silent. Ned could hear the wind and waves and the shouts of some far-away children, and began to sweat. After a few agonizing seconds, a big man who was seated in the center of the patio stared at Ned in the eyes. Without averting his glance, he asked, "So, is this him?"

At that, a woman who was sitting on the patio's handrail put her brightly colored and fruit-festooned drink down and boozily approached Ned. She stopped about six inches away from him and focused on his eyes. Ned could smell her breath. She was in her mid forties, and her eyes came up to his lips despite her high heels. She had a big pile of harshly dyed hair on top of her head and wore a black leather jacket over a pink tank top and jeans. She grinned.

"So, is it him?" the beery fat man barked again.

She grinned again. "I think so," she answered without taking her eyes off Ned, but not registering much focus.

"Waddaya mean you think so?" shouted the man angrily. "Didn't you say you fucked the guy?"

She shrugged and let out a bit of a laugh. "Yeah, yeah, but there were lots of guys that night and I was—well—I was really drunk."

"You're drunk *now*, you stupid whore," said the big man with an exasperated smile. "How can you tell for sure? You want me to take his pants off?"

"No, but if you take his shirt off, I could look at his tats."

Another man, thin and sinister-looking with a shaved head, got up and approached Ned, who had done nothing but stand and breathe since his arrival. "That's a pretty fuckin' good idea," he said. "That way we can see if he's traveling light or not." Ned didn't know if that meant whether they wanted to know if he was armed or wearing a wire. But he stopped thinking about it when he saw that the thin man had a sawed-off shotgun under his jacket, and it was pointed at Ned's head.

It was at that point he realized he had not brought a gun with him. He looked around for Semyon, who was sitting in a chair just off from the main group. He was staring at Ned expectantly, and not quite smiling. He was not, as Ned had hoped, coming to his rescue.

"You heard the man," barked the leader. "Take off your shirt, slim."

Ned did as he was told. The woman in front of him nodded. "Yep, it's him," she said. "He's got the JHAP tat there on his arm, only one of the Sons in Arizona to get it—punishment for crapping his pants at a warehouse robbery." She laughed and said to Ned, "How ya been, Tiger?"

Ned couldn't help sighing with relief, but he still didn't answer the woman who was now openly flirting with him. The fat man got up and approached him, inspecting his torso. Eventually he smiled. "Nice Sons tat," he said. "I see your entry date, but no exit date."

"I'm not officially out yet," Ned croaked.

The fat man laughed. "From what I heard, I'd say you were," he said. "You better get something done about that—the Sons find you with a tat like this and they'll fuck you up pretty bad."

"I don't think the tattoo is why they want to fuck me up," Ned said with the best smile he could muster.

The fat man laughed and offered him a seat. He also told the other man to put the shotgun away. He did, but he appeared reluctant to do so and fixed a hateful glare at Ned. Ned put his shirt back on and sat. The fat man told the drunk woman to get Ned a beer. She went into the bar without a word.

"I'm Pervert, that's Bear, this is Donnie, that's Ian the Turtle, that's Greasy Dan and you've already met Otto." Ned shook hands with Pervert and Bear, who was sitting next to him, and nodded at the others as they were introduced. Otto, the thin man who had the idea to take Ned's shirt off was the only one who did not nod back or at least smile. "Sorry 'bout the unpleasant greeting, but you can't be too careful," he said. "When Simon here asked me if I knew you," he indicated he was talking about Semyon. "I could only tell him that I knew *of* you, but when your name came up Proud Mary told me about the party in Flagstaff, so I told him we could find out if you really were who you said you were."

Ned smiled. "Who else would I be?"

"Well, if you were a cop, you'd be a dead cop by now," Pervert said with a laugh.

Otto, who wasn't laughing, added, "Or a dead rat."

"Aw, shuddup Otto," Pervert snapped, then turned back to Ned. "He's our resident conspiracy theorist. He says that the fact you're still alive shows that you must have been working with the cops."

"Really?" Ned said and stared at Otto, mustering the toughest look he could. "Is that so?"

"Yeah, but my sister's ex-husband is with the feds and I checked with him," Pervert said. "You don't have any pig friends, the Sons just haven't caught up to you yet." He laughed. "Which confirms my own personal theory that the Sons are pretty damn stupid."

As they were laughing, Proud Mary returned with a Coors Light for Ned and something bright blue and frozen for herself. She put them down on the table in front of Ned and sat in his lap, placed her arms around him and absent-mindedly began nuzzling his neck, cheek and ear.

"Get the fuck outta here, Mary!" shouted Pervert as he cuffed her in the head. "Men are talking."

With that, Mary slunk away and sat, dejected-looking, in a chair next to Semyon.

"Anyways, now that you're cool with Simon and his buddies, you're cool with us . . . and anyone who pisses on the Sons and gets away with it is okay by me," Pervert smiled. "You can stay the night if you want, we have some cabins on the other side of the road we use sometimes."

Ned realized he was safe for now, but didn't want to push it. He looked over at Semyon for support, but he was busy making out with Mary. Ned paused and told Pervert that he normally would, but he wanted to get the package back to Grigori as soon as possible.

"We'll worry about that later."

After a few beers, Ned began to feel comfortable and had a good time talking with the guys. They spoke about bikes and the differences between the laws in Arizona and the laws in Maryland. Ned didn't know much about Arizona, but he didn't think any of these guys did either, so he was able to bullshit his way through without any opposition.

When Semyon, who had left with Mary, returned, he asked Ned if he was ready to go. "Yeah, I guess, but you gotta drive, I'm getting pretty drunk," Ned lied.

"Of course I drive, it's my car," Semyon snapped back uncharacteristically. "C'mon, let's go, don't forget the package."

Ned looked at Pervert and said; "Oh, yeah, the package. Where is it?"

"It's in my truck. Let's go." Pervert got up and led them all to the parking lot. Ned noticed that all the other guys came with them. Mary was in the dark bar chatting with the bartender. Pervert led them to the pickup in the parking lot and opened the passenger door. He dug around under the seat and pulled out two manila envelopes, one thick and one thin. As he was bent over, Ned could see he had a handgun in his jacket. Pervert handed Ned the two envelopes and said, "The big one's for Greg and his buddies in Detroit and the little one's for you and your little friend there."

Ned thanked him and told him it was a pleasure to do business with him. Pervert smiled and told him that if he was ever in the area, he was always welcome at Mickey's. Ned shook his hand.

Back in the car, Semyon asked Ned if he was really drunk. "No," he answered. "I just wanted them to think I'd had a good time."

Semyon rolled his eyes.

"Looked like you had a good time back there."

Semyon smiled. "I guess so," he said, "but I know what's better. Open our envelope."

Ned did. Inside was a pile of cash. Ned counted it. "There's $2,241," he said. "You can keep the extra dollar."

"How kind."

"Anything else?"

"Yep, a dime bag," Ned showed him.

"Weed?" Semyon sneered. "Fuckin' cheapskates." Then he said something angry in what Ned took to be Uzbek because it didn't sound like any Russian he had heard.

"Oh, come on, it's a nice gesture."

"You can have it."

"I will, thank you."

"You can enjoy it on the way to Detroit."

"Detroit? That's more than a thousand miles from here and it's already five in the afternoon."

"So?"

"So I have to be at work Monday morning."

"Call in sick."

"I can't."

"Fuck your job, you work for Grigori now. He'll pay you way more, three times as much for half the work."

"I know, I know. It's just that I need my job."

Semyon stopped by the side of the road and looked at Ned angrily. "And exactly why do you need your phony-baloney job so bad?"

Ned thought as quickly as he could. "Health insurance."

Semyon laughed. "Don't worry, man, Grigori will take care of you."

While that should have been reassuring, Ned could only think about how he was going to explain his unscheduled day off to Dave.

Chapter Five

Ned got comfortable in the passenger seat of Semyon's Lexus because he knew he'd be sitting in it for quite a while. As they merged onto Interstate 50, he told Semyon that if they shared the driving, they could save a lot of time. Semyon was reluctant at first, but finally gave in, suggesting they change after a dinner break. Ned smiled and agreed, reclined in the passenger seat and closed his eyes. Although he expected Semyon to understand that he intended to get some sleep, he didn't. Instead, he just kept talking.

"So the Lawbreakers really like you, eh?"

Ned tried at first to show a little aggravation in an attempt to convey a hint to Semyon, but gave up after realizing it would never work. "I guess so. They seem very open to the idea of doing business with me . . . I mean, with us."

"Oh, they love to do business with us. We always deliver, have fair prices," Semyon said, then paused. "And we are white, which seems to be very important to Lawbreakers—they really don't like black people or Mexicans."

"Yeah, that's the way it is with lots of bikers," Ned replied. The look on Semyon's face indicated he wanted a little more explanation. "They'll work with blacks and Mexicans when they absolutely have to, but they never trust them."

"But white people all treated the same—Polish, Swedish, Italian?"

Ned had never thought about it before. "I guess so. I mean, it's different if someone is an immigrant, like you guys—no offense—because he's not an American, but generally, yeah, I mean, you might call an Italian guy a 'wop' or make a Polish joke, but that stuff's kind of died out over the years."

Semyon looked pensive.

"Is that not how it is with you guys?"

Semyon laughed. "No. Stupid Americans."

Ned didn't want to pursue it any further, but he knew Semyon would tell him anyway. "What do you mean 'stupid'?"

"Well, I say stupid because you Americans think the rest of the world works the same way you do—the famous 'American way'—or the rest of the world can just piss off."

"Honestly, we generally don't care how the rest of the world works."

"That's not just stupid, it's criminal."

Ned sighed, and said, "Okay, smart guy, name some of the important streets in New York City."

"Broadway, 42nd Street, Fifth Avenue . . ."

"Okay, now name some of the important streets in Tulsa, Oklahoma."

"How the hell would I know the streets in Tulsa? I don't even know where Tulsa is."

"Well, that's how Americans see the world. If it's important enough, we already know about it and if it isn't, it isn't."

Semyon laughed despite himself. "Very good, we say the same thing of Russians," he said. "They don't care about other countries until they start shooting the Russians."

"But you're Russian," Ned said. "You were born and raised in Russia, so was your dad. That makes you Russian."

"Nope, I am Uzbek," Semyon said solemnly. "Does a black man suddenly turn white if he lives in America for three generations?"

"No, but he is still an American."

"This is not what your friends in the Lawbreakers would say."

Ned couldn't help but laugh and admit that Semyon had a point.

When Semyon got tired of driving, they stopped for dinner at a roadside diner in Frederick, Maryland. They spoke over dinner. Ned found that he was beginning to like talking to Semyon, except for the giggle, which he still found annoying.

Over steaks, french fries and beer, the two talked about how they got to where they are now. Ned recounted the basics of his own story, but set it in Arizona instead of Springfield. He spoke about how he was doing poorly in school and how his aunt's ex-boyfriend got him started selling drugs. Then he told him about how everything just kind of happened around him until he found himself a full-patch member of the Sons of Satan.

Semyon nodded and, between bites, said he understood. But Ned could tell he was just biding his time until he could tell his own story. When Ned was done, Semyon pushed his plate away and leaned both elbows onto the table. Then he took a deep breath and said, "I will tell you how entire region of Eastern Europe and Central Asia has become all organized crime."

Ned settled in. He knew Semyon was going to tell him whether he liked it or not. But he was kind of interested in the subject, so he didn't mind at all.

"You are too young to remember the Cold War, right?"

Ned said he was, but that he kind of understood the basic story.

Semyon shrugged and continued. "Okay, west of line is Capitalist, east of line is Communist, right?" He explained using the forks and knives on the table to make a line separating his plate and his beer glass. "Nothing passes over line, or at least very little."

Ned agreed. "Because of this, we on east side have very little crime; without anything worth stealing, there is nothing to steal," Semyon continued, trying to sound philosophical. "Besides, there is no way to get away with it. Party is people and people is Party—someone sees you have more than them, they tell on you. It's like you stole from them, even if you didn't."

"But that all changed when we were kids, right?"

"Yes. In 1989, 1990, some republics in and around Soviet Union decided they no longer want to be dominated by Soviets, they open up their borders to the West and Western products."

"But that's good, right?" Ned asked. "I mean, you want to trade for Western products, don't you?"

Semyon rolled his eyes. "This is why we think you are stupid. You see everything as simple, good or bad, but everything is good and bad," he said with a snort. "Of course we want Western products, but we can't pay for them."

"Why not?" Ned asked. "I thought the whole point of Communism was that you all had jobs."

"Look at it this way—when border is closed, Bulgarians buy Bulgarian shoes because that's all they can get, then border opens, one man buys Nikes and suddenly every woman in town wants to sleep with him. You can't fight that kind of thing. Then everyone in town sells everything they can to get a pair of Nikes."

"So then you have an entire Bulgarian town of poor people with nice shoes?"

"Yes, and since nobody wants Bulgarian shoes anymore, factory closes, and everyone in town is out of work," Semyon said. "Now they have nice shoes and nothing to eat."

"Really? Nobody saw it coming?"

"Nope, the wanting of shoes is too great—and it's not just Bulgaria, it is every country between Germany and China."

"So then what happened?"

"Well, Westerners came in selling their shoes, and we sold what we had."

"Which was?"

"Women."

"What?"

"Women," Semyon said, as though he was speaking of any other commodity. "At first, they would do it themselves, offer sex to Western businessmen by the side of the road for next to nothing—they had no idea of what it was worth—and many get beaten up or even killed."

"Really?"

"Yes, so they seek the protection of strong men," Semyon continued. "What you call a pimp. Some countries, the biggest part of their economy is based on women and girls selling sex to foreigners."

"Like Moldova?"

"Yes," Semyon looked surprised. "For years, nothing but women and pornos came out of Moldova. How do you know about a sleazy little hole like Moldova and not know about the glorious nation of Uzbekistan?"

"I used to run a strip bar," Ned replied nonchalantly. "If the dancers weren't from Quebec, they were from Moldova."

Semyon giggled. "So you know what I mean. Eventually," he said with what Ned took to be an air of pride, "the pimps got smart and started selling higher-profit products like hashish, heroin and even weapons to the same customers. They banded together, became gangsters, made millions, many millions of dollars."

"And wear Nikes."

"Even worse, even if a man in Bulgarian town has a job, it literally takes him years to afford Nikes," Semyon said. "But his old friend the gangster drives a Bentley, has a herd of women, has everything. He could buy a Nike factory, let alone the shoes."

"What about the police, the government?"

Semyon laughed. "The police are a joke. They make less money than the poor guy who mops up the McDonald's floor—they don't risk their lives for their jobs, they look in another direction. And the government? It's made up primarily of the gangsters' friends and family—or the gangsters themselves."

"So everyone from Germany to China is a gangster or a prostitute?"

"Of course not, but a huge number of them are," Semyon sighed. "And they are everywhere—government, police, everywhere."

"Seems sad, really."

Semyon's face changed. It was the first time Ned had seen him genuinely angry. "How can you talk like this?" he sneered. "You are worse—*pfeh*, American gangster—why did you join the Sons of Satan? Want to make a quick buck instead of going to school? Maybe some girl liked the sound of your big rumbly motorbike?"

Ned couldn't help smile at how perceptive Semyon was. Semyon's face lightened. "Okay, fine, I guess it's all relative. We all want the same thing—lots of money for no work. We are gangsters because we are lazy men."

They both laughed and clinked their beer glasses together in something of a toast. "I can't have too many more of these if I'm gonna drive tonight," warned Ned.

"No, we'll stay here tonight."

"Aren't we in a hurry?"

"I'm never in a hurry. Besides, I have a friend here."

"Really?"

"I have friends everywhere."

After dinner, the pair headed across the street to a low-slung motel. Semyon appeared to know the guy behind the counter who handed Semyon two keys with large plastic key rings after some passing chit-chat.

Ned hoped he'd be surprised with a clean, comfortable room, but he wasn't. The bed was covered in a madly patterned bedspread he knew was intended to hide stains. The bed creaked when he sat on it, and gave a plastic-like sound when he shifted position.

He looked around and was about to turn on the ancient TV when Semyon came in the door Ned had carelessly left unlocked. "You should be more careful, man. I could have been anyone." Ned noticed he had a six-pack of beer and a bottle of vodka in his hands. "It's time to party, man!"

"Nah, man, it's like one in the morning and I am beat," Ned said. The stress of the day had taken a toll on him and he really felt a need to relax.

"You Americans are babies," Semyon said with obvious disappointment. "Okay, I'll go, but tomorrow night we party."

"Yeah, yeah, sure thing. Good night, Semyon."

"Good night, sleepy."

Ned made sure the door was locked after Semyon left and went back to the TV. He was dozing off in an armchair when he heard a knock at the door. He bolted to the window to see who it was. He couldn't see. Whoever it was knocked again. The old door didn't have a peephole, so he opened it a crack. On the other side was a tall black woman in shorts and a tube top. She had a long face that looked like she had seen some hard times.

"You with Simon? Your friend Simon called me and said you needed a date," she said. "So here I am."

Ned stammered, and the laughed. "He did, did he?" he finally said while opening the door wider. Ned was actually both bored and lonely but lots of things about this woman made him uneasy. "Well, I'll tell him thanks tomorrow, but I'm really not feeling very well and really just want to get some sleep."

"I got just the thing for you," she said and stepped past him and into the room. "I'll make you feel all better."

Ned started to get nervous. "No, really, I'm actually quite sick, and I don't think it'd be fair to give it to you," he looked at her face to see if she believed him. Then, after a long pause, he asked, "Did he already pay you?"

She sat down in the armchair facing him still holding the door. "Yeah. Yeah, he did," she said with a blank look. "I was supposed to be something of a gift I guess."

Ned smiled and approached her. "Well, it's the thought that counts," and realizing that could be construed as insulting, he added. "And I really appreciate your coming out. Can I give you a little something for your trouble?" He handed her a pair of twenties.

She grinned generously, then stood up and kissed him on the cheek. "You take care of yourself, baby," she told him and started towards the door, before turning around. "Oh, and Simon asked me to tell you that I wasn't from Quebec or from some other place I can't remember, Mongolia or something."

Ned laughed and thanked her again. He locked the door after she left and rolled a joint to relax.

* * *

Ned woke up to Semyon's insistent knocking and shouting. He was surprised to see that it was almost noon. He opened the door and his new friend let himself in. Semyon was grinning conspiratorially. "Now we get started!" he announced. "After we dine."

. They didn't get back onto the road until well past one o'clock, despite Ned complaining about the long drive they had in front of them.

When they arrived at the building where Ned had first met Grigori and his men, it was dark, but Ned could see that many of the same cars were parked out front. The watcher in the BMW got out of his car this time and greeted Semyon warmly. Semyon introduced him to Ned as Pyotr.

Semyon walked up to the door. He had drawn a crude face sticking its tongue out on the envelope and held it in front of the video camera when he pressed the intercom button. After he was acknowledged, he said, "Open up, it's the FBI." Whoever was on the other side groaned and said something in Russian. The only word Ned could make out was Semyon's name. Then he heard the door unlock.

Semyon led him inside. It didn't look much like he remembered, but the last time he was there he had only paid attention to the basement. While the basement was stark and even putrid, the main floor was clean and looked very much like the abandoned factory it was. Had it not been in an abandoned section of Detroit, Ned thought, some smart developer could transform it into highly desirable condos for the hipster generation.

Ned followed Semyon up a set of stairs and along the hall to a wood and glass door. The word "Chairman" had been painstakingly hand-painted decades ago on the glass in white letters with a gold shadow. Behind it were venetian blinds that had been closed. Semyon knocked and the door was opened.

As Ned walked in, he could hardly believe his eyes. In better times, the chairman's office would have been desirable because of its size, the windows offering a near limitless view and tons of sunshine. But now it had been made out like a sultan's palace. There were clearly expensive—if not entirely tasteful—paintings and tapestries on the wall, a real bearskin rug complete with head, and two sculptures of rearing lions, each painted gold and no less than nine feet high. Between them was an oak desk as big as a small car. And behind it was Grigori, dressed again in an expensive-looking suit and tons of gold. Throughout the room were a few men, some Ned recognized from his time in the basement and some he didn't. They were all standing except one. As he had been when Ned was in the factory's basement, Vasilly was sitting alone in a chair tucked into a corner of the room. He remembered him as the thin man with the gun. His cold, emotionless stare left him feeling a bit cold inside.

Grigori said something in Russian to Semyon and Semyon giggled. Then he replied and handed him the thick envelope. Grigori put it on a pile of others, stood up and approached Ned. Ned couldn't help flinching when Grigori threw his arms around him and gave him a big bear hug. Ned could hear laughter from the rest of the men. Then Grigori offered Ned a seat and went back to his chair behind the desk.

He smiled broadly. "I have plans for you," he said.

Ned did little but look nervous.

Grigori nodded at his own opinion. "You don't mind getting rich, do you?" he asked in a jolly way. "You do like money, don't you?"

Ned smiled and nodded back. "Yes, sir, yes I do."

"Good, good," Grigori said with obvious pride. "Here is your new job." And he handed Ned a piece of paper. On it was printed:

Hawkridge Heating and Cooling Corp.
4915 New Castle Rd.
Wilmington DE19850
Attention: Thor Andersson

"What will I do there?" Ned asked.

"You will be manager of shipping and receiving," Grigori replied. "And also, you will be my main man in Mid-Atlantic region. It is all arranged."

"I have rather specialized experience in shipping and receiving—nothing like this."

Grigori laughed, and the others seemed to get the inside joke, too. "Our whole business—your business— is just shipping and receiving," he said. "Besides, it's very easy job." He went on to describe the position. He told Ned that Hawkridge was one of the country's biggest suppliers of parts and assemblies for heating, ventilation and air-conditioning systems. Andersson, whom Grigori referred to as "the Swede," made his fortune by establishing factories in formerly Communist states long before any other westerners had dared to. While other companies in the industry were still making their parts in the U.S., the Swede was paying less than a fifth for the same parts from factories in Romania, Serbia and places like that. By the time his competition had started outsourcing to China, Hawkridge was already the market leader and was considered the gold standard despite having competitive prices.

Grigori's younger brother Fedor had owned one of the Romanian factories that the Swede purchased from and had come up with the idea of shipping what

Grigori called "our product" with the containers of air-conditioning parts. The products in question were refrigerant coils. Since they were full of Freon and other relatively dangerous chemicals and the Swede had all the necessary permits and licenses, they were routinely left uninspected. Fedor shipped the Swede double the number of coils he ordered, filled half with "their product" instead of refrigerant, then had someone separate the two and distribute the heroin.

It was a lucrative business, with amounts of drugs and money rivaling the legendary French Connection. The key to it, as Grigori saw it, was to make sure that the person receiving the coils would do his job efficiently and quietly—and not take advantage of Grigori's generosity. And in Ned, Grigori believed he had found such a person. He knew the receiver could not be an Eastern European immigrant, couldn't have a significant criminal record, but would have to have a solid understanding of and extensive experience in the drug trade. He also had to be well-spoken, polite and able to hide the appearance of criminality.

Ned couldn't help but agree that Grigori had assessed the Jared-Macnair-posing-as-Eric-Steadman character fairly accurately. But he was presented with a problem. He now had to convince Dave, his FBI case-worker, to allow him to switch jobs. Because he realized that he knew enough that if he backed out now, the Russians would want to get rid of him.

While he was trying to think of a strategy, Grigori snapped his fingers and asked, "There is nothing to think about, you will do this."

"Oh, yeah, yeah, of course," Ned stammered. "It's just a lot to take in all of a sudden like this."

Grigori laughed and said something to Semyon. Semyon giggled and opened a door that Ned took to be a closet. While he was in there, Grigori told Ned that he shouldn't worry, that he would send Semyon with him to make things easy for him. And added that he could use the peace and quiet of having Semyon out of town for a while. In the new job, Ned would be paid a token salary—significantly higher than the mailroom but not high enough to merit suspicion—with benefits, but the real money would come from how much "product" he could supply to Grigori's dealers. Grigori said it would not surprise him if Ned was paid as much as a million dollars in his first year.

Semyon came back out of the adjoining room with a beer for Ned, a bottle of vodka and six small glasses. He distributed the vodka to all the men in the room, although Ned noticed that Vasilly declined his. Grigori then said a few words and raised his glass. Everyone in the room except Vasilly followed suit. Then he and all the others downed their vodka in a single gulp. Ned took a swing of beer. Grigori smiled broadly.

Semyon made a gesture to Ned that indicated it was time to go. The other men in the room had started talking among themselves. When Ned stood up, so did Grigori. The room fell silent. Grigori smiled, his gold teeth briefly flashing a reflection of sunlight. "Go, Macnair, and make us lots of money." All of the men in the room except Vasilly laughed.

* * *

After the meeting, Ned and Semyon got into the Lexus. Semyon looked at Ned and asked, "So what do you think?"

Ned fought for the right words. "I'd say I'm impressed. I'm very impressed."

"You should be! Grigori has set you up to be very, very rich and all you have to do is shake some hands and open a few packages."

"Yeah, that's the picture I get too," Ned replied, unable to suppress a smile. "One thing, though. What was that Grigori said when he toasted?"

Semyon giggled. "I can't remember exactly, but it was something like 'God guide this stupid American and let him succeed and not ever betray us,'" he recalled. "And, of course, 'death to Gypsies.'"

"What?"

Semyon looked confused for a second. "Oh—the 'death to Gypsies' thing," then he giggled. "That's something he must have picked up in Romania. They all say that. So do the Bulgarians and I think also the Slovaks, but I can't be sure, anywhere where there are Gypsies. I don't think they mean anything by it, kind of like if Jew might hit his thumb with a hammer and says 'Jesus Christ!' Just an expression."

"But what's so bad about Gypsies?"

"People over there say all kinds of bad things about them," he said, "but I don't get into it because I am kind of like a Gypsy. I'm an Uzbek who has never seen Uzbekistan, I was born and grew up in Russia but am not Russian and now I live in America but am not American. But Europeans, especially in the East, are not like me or like you. Unless your great-great-great-grandfather fought the Turks a thousand years ago to defend your village, you will always be an outsider who is not to be trusted, even to be hated—and Gypsies, by definition, are always from someplace else."

Ned was mulling this over when Semyon turned onto a side street, then another. Finally he pulled into a driveway beside a nice low bungalow, which was brightly lit given how late it was. As they got out of the car, Semyon kicked a tricycle that was in his path into the yard and swore in what was probably Russian.

He opened the unlocked door without knocking, entered a small vestibule and was suddenly pounced on by four children ranging in age from toddler to about six. He said something to them in Russian and they all dispersed. As they were detaching themselves from Semyon, Ned noticed a woman appear from inside the house with her hands on her hips. She was short and thick with short black hair that had been artificially curled but poorly maintained. She was dressed in a sleeveless black sweater and patterned pink-and-white Capri pants and topped off her Midwestern retro-chic look with thick, black plastic glasses. She started shouting something in Russian at Semyon.

"English, please, honey, we have a guest," Semyon said calmly, gesturing at Ned.

The woman put her lips together in an angry pout and forced air through her nose. "Fine!" she said. "Where have you been, don't you know the baby is still asleep and who the fuck is this?"

Semyon laughed. "My beloved wife Ludmilla, this is Macnair. Macnair, this is Ludmilla, my beloved wife."

Ludmilla softened and smiled at Ned, offering her hand. "Pleased to meet you Macnair, welcome to our home." Before he could shake her hand, she went back to yelling at Semyon in Russian. But he just shrugged and grabbed Ned by the arm and led him into the living room.

It was a fairly normal living room, but very messy with the kids and their stuff, and Ned noticed that much of the furniture was low and without normal chair backs. Much of the wall space was covered with framed black-and-white photos, which Ned correctly surmised were the result of Ludmilla's hobby.

Semyon shooed a pair of small giggling children off the couch and offered Ned a seat. He sat on the other end of the low sofa and said something in Russian. Ned noticed that all four of the children were staring at him and would not look away no matter what he did. They all looked like Semyon only with rounder faces and bigger eyes and although Ned identified them all as boys, because they all had the same salad-bowl haircut, he couldn't be sure.

Ludmilla returned with a bottle of vodka and three glasses. She explained that she was Russian and met Semyon when her family moved into his neighborhood after her dad was killed. They married young, but didn't have children until they had their future figured out. When Semyon had a chance to move to America, they jumped at the chance.

Ned noticed that the kids were falling asleep around them, and Ludmilla told him that her parents were so strict with her that she no longer believed in artificial constructs like set bedtimes and specific bedrooms. Either she warmed to Ned or the vodka took effect. Ludmilla—or Millie, as her American friends called her—told Ned that she was a full-time mom, but also had a part-time job teaching photography at a local community college. "I'm a real woman," she pointed out proudly. "Not one of those skinny, coked-up airheads Semyon's gangster friends always have with them."

It took Ned some time to work up the courage to ask Ludmilla where he could sleep. She smiled and took him into a room with two empty twin beds. Ned couldn't remember if he'd traveled into another time zone, so just to be safe, he set the alarm on his cell phone for seven o'clock.

Just as he was falling asleep, he saw Semyon—shirtless and drunk—stumble into the room. The first thing Ned noticed was how many tattoos Semyon had and how intricate they were. Semyon fell into the bed beside Ned and put an arm around his neck. "We are friends now," Semyon said and Ned noticed that his accent was much thicker. "So we keep each other's secrets."

"Sure, man, sure."

"And even though Ludmilla calls my friends 'gangsters,' she does not know," he said. "She thinks I sell used, maybe stolen, auto parts, but she knows nothing about drugs or guns or women or nothing, you know?"

"I understand."

Semyon rubbed Ned's hair affectionately. "I know, I know, you are good man, you are not like us, but you are one of us, you are okay, I love you." And at that, he worked very hard to stand up and stumbled out of the room. Ned could see that he had a large handgun in his right hand. In fact, he accidentally banged it against the door on the way out and giggled his now-familiar giggle.

Ned drifted off to sleep.

Chapter Six

Ned felt the vibration before he heard the "peep peep peep" of his cell-phone alarm. He really wanted to shut it off and roll back over and go back to sleep, but he knew how important his next call would be. As he straightened up and rolled over, he accidentally stepped on one of the two young children who had fallen asleep on the floor of his room some time during the night. The kid didn't wake up, just rolled over and let out a long sigh.

Ned headed for the kitchen. The house was quiet. Ned leaned against the fridge and hit the contact for "Shithead." After a couple of rings, Ned felt relieved when he heard the phone transfer over to voice mail.

He waited through Neil's long and overly complicated message, then said, "Neil, it's Eric, I can't come to work today . . . uh . . . I'm really fucked up, terrible headaches and vomiting . . . I really shouldn't come in."

He hung up, rubbed his eyes and looked for an unoccupied place to go back to sleep, as one of the floor children had since invaded his bed. He curled up on the living-room sofa and fell back asleep. About thirty minutes passed before his phone rang. The display said "Shithead." Ned hit ignore. Five minutes later, it rang again, flashing "Shithead." Ned picked up. Before he could say hello, he heard Neil, his boss at the mailroom, screaming. "Eric, you ignorant fuck, get your ass into work today," he raged. "I don't care how bad your hangover is. I have a department to run and I don't need your laziness to get in the way."

Ned waited for him to finish. "Neil, I really am sick, there's literally no way I could come in today," Ned said. "I may have something contagious."

"Maybe I should be the judge of that," Neil said. "Why don't you come in, and I'll decide how sick you are . . . send you home if you're telling the goddamned truth."

"Are you nuts?" Ned was angry now, and his head really was pounding. "What kind of slave-driver are you? It's the law that you gotta allow me a sick day from time to time—and it's not like I've ever asked for one before."

"Listen, you lying bag of crap, you could be replaced by a fuckin' monkey," Neil scolded. "And if you don't come in, I'll think about doing that." He hung up. Ned couldn't help thinking that Neil had enjoyed their little fight. He tried to go back to sleep, but his headache wouldn't let him. Instead, he lay on the living room couch with his eyes closed, rolling and stretching in a fruitless effort to find a comfortable position on the short sofa.

* * *

When Ned showed up for work Tuesday morning, Neil Bird, the manager, was there to greet him outside the front door. He was a small man, prone to wearing denim in unconventional ways. He shaved his head to hide his baldness, but had a reddish mustache and wire-framed glasses. He had his arms tightly crossed over his chest and he was pacing.

He gave an angry smile when he saw Ned. "You don't look sick to me, Eric," he snapped.

"I'm not anymore," Ned tried to stay upbeat. "Just needed a good day's rest."

"You're a liar," Neil said. "I'm keeping my eye on you, and if you slip up . . ."

Ned was exasperated. "What is your fucking problem, man?" he asked, shaking his head. "One sick day and you're making a federal case out of it—and you really shouldn't talk to me that way."

Neil grinned. "I'll talk to you any way I want. I'm the boss," he said. "And you have to do everything I say."

Ned put his face in his hands. "You know what? Fuck you, Neil."

"Fuck me? Fuck you, you're fired."

"Thank you, Neil," Ned said, shaking his hand. "You've made me the happiest man on Earth. Tell Chuck or Bob to grab my stuff." Then he turned and left. He could hear Neil shouting angrily behind him, but didn't care what he had to say.

* * *

Back at home, Ned got a phone call from Dave. "You got fired? You got fired from the simplest fuckin' job in the entire world?" he asked. "What kind of a moron are you?" He didn't wait for Ned to answer. "Wait . . . here it is. You were fired for 'massive insubordination'—so you're an asshole, not a moron."

Ned sighed. "Dave, let me explain . . ."

"Explain when you see me at Walt's—tonight." He hung up.

Ned thought for a moment and called Semyon. He told him that he'd been fired and that he needed to see the Swede that day.

"So see him," Semyon said. "You have the address."

Ned was really taken aback. "You mean I should just go . . . with no introduction or anything?"

"Yeah, man, he knows who you are."

After thanking Semyon for letting him stay over at his house and praising Ludmilla and the kids, Ned hung up and took a shower. He no longer owned a suit, but put on a pressed shirt, tan trousers and a sports coat.

The Hawkridge factory was not too far from where Ned lived. Officially in the city of Wilmington, but really out in the boonies, the factory didn't look like what Ned had pictured. Instead of a huge gray building with smokestacks like he remembered from the Midwest, Hawkridge looked very much like a warehouse. It was a rectangular red brick building with tinted windows and a few dozen cars of varying value parked out front.

When he went in he greeted the receptionist. When she asked him why he was there, he pulled the paper out of his jacket pocket and said, "I'm here to see Thor Andersson."

"Take a seat, he'll just be a few moments," she smiled. "And, if you want to impress him, he pronounces his name like 'Tor' not 'Thor.'"

"Thanks," Ned said and smiled back. "I'll remember that."

He was leafing through the old magazines when the office door opened. Two men came out, obviously still discussing business. Ned correctly surmised that the man in the suit was selling something, but the big guy in the jeans wasn't buying. He was about Ned's height but thicker. He had closely cropped graying hair and small blue eyes with high-set eyebrows that gave him something of a surprised look, no matter what his expression.

He smiled at Ned and asked if he was there about the shipping and receiving job. Ned said he was and Andersson led him in. The office was nice and well lit, if somewhat stark. The furniture was small, modest and wooden but comfortable. Andersson shook Ned's hand and introduced himself. Ned actually had to stop and think about what name he was going to use with Andersson. Then he reminded himself that he was going to try to clear it by Dave, so he introduced himself as Eric Steadman.

Andersson explained that the position was as shipping and receiving manager. Ned would oversee a couple of other employees whose job it was to receive shipments from suppliers, sign for them, get them to the right people and to make sure outgoing shipments were picked up by the right people at the right time. And he would also be personally responsible for any shipments coming from one major supplier—Envoglobal Bucuresti, which Ned correctly surmised was Grigori's brother's factory.

Ned studied the Swede's face for any hint of conspiracy—a nod, a wink, a raised eyebrow or even a sideways look—but saw none. He realized that he had finished talking, and responded by saying, "Sounds like a great job, and I know I can do it." They discussed pay, benefits and hours, and the Swede gave Ned a tour of the factory and introduced him to Juan and Katie, the two clerks he was to supervise.

Ned was impressed by the whole operation, and would have looked forward to working there even if he wasn't part of Grigori's plan. After Neil and the mailroom, working at Hawkridge seemed almost idyllic. He expressed his gratitude to Grigori.

Andersson smiled, shook his head and sighed. "Years ago, Grigori was a very important man in Romania," he said. "And when I went to Romania with the idea of building and exporting things to the West, he's the one that made it happen—he is responsible for where I am today."

Ned smiled.

"I know he has some bad friends, but that's just the way it is over there," the Swede continued. "But he also helps people, and he told me you were a good kid who just needed a break. My instinct tells me he's right—let's hope he is."

On his way home, Ned stopped at the library to use the Internet. He looked up Hawkridge and Andersson and even found out that the chairman of Envoglobal Bucuresti was Fedor Radulov. He searched for Grigori Radulov with many different spellings of Grigori, but only two sites were returned and both were in what might have been Romanian. When he clicked on both of them he saw that they had been blocked by the library's firewall.

He left and went to the coffee shop Dave had arranged to meet him in. Ned hadn't eaten all day, and was starving. His pockets were full of cash, but he didn't want Dave to know it, so he didn't order anything more than coffee while he waited.

When Dave finally arrived, he had a very stern, almost parental look on his face. "What am I gonna do with you?" he asked Ned.

"Nothing," Ned said with a smile. "I've already taken care of it."

"I'll say you have," Dave snapped back. "But the company, my company, is not going to pay you to sit on your ass. You are going to work."

"No, really," Ned said. "I already have a new job."

"What the fuck?" Dave was even angrier upon hearing that. "You can't just go and get yourself another job without my approval."

"I know, I realize that now," Ned said, hoping Dave would feel sympathetic. "But it was such a great opportunity."

"Yeah? I'll be the judge of that," Dave had clearly softened. "And if you think I'm gonna let you be a bouncer or bartender or some other job that puts you in contact with the lifestyle I'm protecting you from, I'll see if they have any openings at the sewage treatment plant or the chicken slaughterhouse out on Route 45."

Ned laughed. "How does shipping and receiving manager sound?" he said proudly. "At Hawkridge."

"Hawkridge? Wow, I know that company," Dave sounded truly impressed. "Very good to their workers, benefits, profit-sharing, even mortgage guarantees for long-term employees."

"Yeah," was all Ned could say.

"So how did you get to know someone in management there?" Dave sounded suspicious now. "And why would they want you—for a management position, no less."

Ned took a moment. "Well, there's this sweet lady at the credit-assessment company, Dolores." Ned grinned at his choice of names because he, in fact, hated Dolores even more than Neil. "She told me that Hawkridge was expanding and looking to hire, so I gave them a call."

Dave, terribly out of character, was at a loss for words.

That night, Ned bought himself a laptop and a big-screen TV.

Chapter Seven

Ned's first morning at Hawkridge was largely uneventful. He had no formal experience in shipping and receiving, so he asked Katie—the woman he was supposed to manage—to show him the ropes. He could tell she knew that he was bullshitting her about any experience in the field, but she played along anyway, and he was surprised that he could sense no resentment from her.

At noon, Katie asked him if he wanted to go to lunch with her, Juan and some of the other office staff. Ned declined. He didn't want to appear as though he needed to be with them all the time. But he did feel like a bite to eat and he hadn't packed anything, so he walked outside after they had left.

He wasn't even out the door when he heard it: Semyon's crazy Russian (or maybe Uzbek?) disco blaring through the open windows of his now-familiar neon green Lexus. Immediately, Ned walked as quickly as he could to the car. When Semyon saw him, he pushed hard on the horn as though his audacious car and deafening music had somehow escaped Ned's notice. He was all smiles as Ned opened the passenger door and jumped in. He was less pleased when Ned's first move once inside the car was to turn the music down to a thumping and blipping murmur.

"Hey, hey, man!" Semyon shouted. "You could get killed for that in Moscow."

Ned gave him a look that he hoped contained the message for Semyon to get serious. "What are you doing here?" he asked.

Semyon didn't answer, instead he pulled away from the curb with smoking tires. "Subtle," Ned said.

"What does that 'subtle' word mean, anyway?"

Ned was about to explain when he sighed and said, "I would tell you, but I still don't think you'd understand."

Semyon smiled passively and drove them to a small public green space with a picnic table. Semyon took a canvas bag out of the trunk. When he got to the table, he brought out two orders of cheeseburgers and fries from a fast-food outlet Ned had never heard of before, a big bottle of vodka, a glass, a can of cheap beer and a small metal object. He tossed it to Ned as soon as he pulled it out of the bag.

"What is this thing?" Ned examined the device. It was a matte black metal tube with a straight six-inch shaft. The tube then doubled back over itself again and again until it formed sort of a square. Two metal rods had been welded to it which Ned guessed were to keep it rigid. It had some tiny white letters and numbers on it, probably a product code. Each end of the tube had a silver-colored stopper stamped onto it.

"You should know; it's your job to ship and receive them," Semyon smiled. "It's a coolant coil from an industrial-sized air conditioner . . . well, it's part of one, at least . . . Hawkridge can make air conditioners any size because coolant coils are modular. They can use one or a million, turn them on or off. Saves energy somehow." Then he dove into his cheeseburger.

Ned turned the coil over in his hands. It was a simple thing, really, but he could tell they required some work to manufacture. "So what do I have to do with them?"

"Well, you will order double the number of coils Hawkridge needs from Envoglobal in Romania," he said between bites. "Then you will ship half to a subcontractor called Premier Solutions in Detroit."

"Grigori's company?"

"A mutual friend of ours."

Ned liked the simplicity of the plan. "So, how do I know which ones to send to Detroit?"

Semyon put up his index finger to indicate that he would answer after he was finished chewing. When he did, he reached back into the canvas bag and pulled out another coil, which appeared to be identical to the first. Then he tossed it to Ned who caught it without dropping the first one. "Notice anything different?"

"No." Ned was spinning it around to inspect it and then stopped. "Yeah, yeah I do, this one has yellow letters and numbers on it and the other one has white."

"Very smart."

"Very subtle."

"I thought you'd say that."

* * *

Back at the office, Ned was about to start his job in earnest when the phone on his desk rang. He wasn't sure what the correct protocol for answering it was, so he just said hello.

A heavily accented voice on the other side responded without saying hello. "Roman is having second thoughts," It said. "He says he will have to meet you."

"Who's Roman? Who are you?"

"It will be arranged," the voice continued. "Semyon will have the details." Then he hung up.

* * *

That evening, after Ned left work, he was surprised to see Semyon's car parked outside his apartment building. Semyon was sitting inside and appeared to be asleep. Ned tapped on the window close to where his head was pressed against it and was shocked that Semyon had drawn a gun and pointed it at him for a second or so.

After he realized what was going on, Semyon apologized and asked to be invited in. Ned accommodated him but did not appreciate his friend's constant patter about how shitty and low-rent all of his possessions were.

When they were finally both sitting down, Semyon told him that Roman was having second thoughts about him and would have to meet him.

"So I've heard," Ned answered.

Semyon smiled. "This is serious, man," he said. "Roman is key, he's important, you have to do this."

"Or what?"

"You will lose your job," he answered. Then after a long pause, he added, "At the very least."

Ned chuckled mirthlessly. "Okay, let's go meet Roman."

"Okay, I'll put together a meeting in the next few days and you can take a couple of days off work . . ."

"A couple of days?"

"Yeah, Roman is in New York—Brooklyn," Semyon said. "It'll be an overnight trip."

Ned didn't think getting time off from Hawkridge would be a problem, but keeping it a secret from Dave would prove harder. He thought about it for a second, and realized the best way to stay out of trouble would be to limit Semyon's involvement. "Well, I have two conditions."

"You are in no position to make conditions."

"Too bad," he said. "The trip is not over a Friday—and I drive."

Semyon laughed. "The Friday thing is fine. I don't want to ruin a weekend, either," he said. "But I am not riding in your piece-of-shit car and I don't want you driving mine."

"We can rent one. Do you have any cash?"

Semyon shrugged and pulled a roll of twenties as thick around as a coffee mug and showed Ned. "Some, but there are lots of things to do in New York."

* * *

Ned had Semyon pick him up at Hawkridge at eleven o'clock on Monday morning. He did not feel like hearing Semyon drone on about how bad his place was again so he waited outside. Semyon had rented an immense SUV, and looked like he hadn't quite managed to learn how to navigate it in tight traffic just yet.

Ned took the wheel and told Semyon he was surprised there was no loud music playing. Semyon looked annoyed and muttered something about satellite radio.

By the time they got on I-95, Semyon had already started his now-familiar chattering. He was complaining about Ludmilla's brother. He was an obese alcoholic who had always given Semyon a hard time for not being Russian, and now he is demanding that they sponsor him for a Green Card. "Fuckin' Russians," Semyon muttered in what Ned noticed was for his benefit because it was in English. "Think they know everything."

Ned snorted. "You work with Russians, your wife is Russian, I sometimes think I'm the only non-Russian you know."

Semyon smiled and looked bemused. "No, there are a few Uzbeks in Dearborn who get together every once in a while," he said. "You would like them, much nicer people than Russians."

"So who's this guy we're going to see . . . Roman, is it?" Ned asked even though he knew the man's name.

"Yeah, Roman," Semyon said. "He's not too bad. Likes to show off his money and that's okay with me because I love it when someone else is paying."

"Yeah, but who is he? Why do I have to meet him?" Ned asked. "Haven't you guys checked me out enough already?"

Semyon put on something of a pensive pout. "Roman did not become who he is by trusting people he does not know," he said. "I know you are trustworthy, Grigori knows you are trustworthy, but Roman, he likes to do things his way. And you had better—as you people say—play ball."

Ned wanted to ask what Semyon meant by that, but didn't feel like being threatened again. "But why is Roman so important?"

Semyon sighed. "I am under orders to let you know as little as possible," he said with what Ned recognized as pretended anger. "Why can't you just be happy shipping packages and making lots of money?"

"I am," Ned replied. "But I'm the one who has to meet and impress this guy, so I'd like to know a little about him to prepare."

Semyon made a big show of knitting his eyebrows and sighed audibly. "Okay, okay, but you tell nobody what I am about to tell you," he finally said. "Grigori was a good Communist. He worked in the Russian embassy in Romania for years and years, and when things started to change there in the 1980s, he made a lot of money selling exit visas to people who wanted to get out of the country. By the time Ceauşescu and his wife were shot, Grigori was already a rich man."

"Ceauşescu?"

"Yes, the communist leader of Romania who was shot by his own people in 1989," Semyon continued. "After he was gone, the whole country went wild."

"And Grigori left?"

"No way! Grigori was way too smart for that," Semyon said, as though Ned had said something too ridiculous to even warrant an answer. "He was by that time a very rich man in a very poor and disorganized country, so he could have whatever he wanted. He bought a bunch of factories—but he put them in his brothers' names because it would look bad for a party member to own so much property and because many questions would be asked back in Moscow."

"So Russia was still communist at that point?"

"Yeah, for a little while," Semyon said. "So Grigori had to continue at his job selling visas while his brothers set up the factories."

"And that's how he met the Swede?"

"Yeah, even before Ceauşescu was killed, Romania encouraged trade with other countries and the Swedes were the first ones in . . . they usually are," Semyon said as though that addendum was supposed to be significant to Ned. "Grigori just kept getting richer and richer, and when the communists fell in Russia, he came back to Moscow and made some even richer friends."

"Richer?"

"Yes, how can I put this? Grigori drives a most expensive Mercedes-Benz, his friends back in Russia have a custom-built Lamborghini for a few weeks until they get bored of it and then get something else," he said. "You should see their houses, they are palaces. Truly."

"And Roman is one of them?"

Semyon laughed. "No, no, no, Roman is like Grigori, but the bosses like him better, so he is in Brooklyn, while Grigori is stuck in Detroit. He is also very jealous of Dimitri in Los Angeles."

Ned smiled. "So if I am Grigori's employee, why do I have to pass Roman's inspection?"

"Because Wilmington is officially in Roman's territory—east coast, you know," Semyon said, as though explaining the situation to an obstinate five year old. "Grigori is only getting away with it because it was such a smart idea and because Roman is getting a generous allowance. But nothing happens until Roman gets on board—and he won't be until he meets you."

They had been driving for hours and had passed by Philadelphia, Camden and Trenton and were traveling at exactly the speed limit through small-town New Jersey when Semyon pulled out his now-familiar bottle of vodka. Ned was so shocked he almost swerved into a car passing him on the left. After recovering with much screaming from his brakes and tires, Ned asked Semyon, "What the fuck are you doing? You can't just open up a bottle of vodka in the front seat of a moving car! We could both go to jail."

"What? Really? I knew you couldn't drink and drive in this country, but I'm not the one driving." He sounded very sheepish by the end of his statement.

Ned, still shaking his head and unable to blink, took the next exit. They eventually ended up on the outskirts of a nice little town called Lawrenceville where Ned stopped at a gas station that had a convenience store attached. "You fill up the tank," he told Semyon. "I'll be back in a sec."

Ned returned with some snacks and other items and put them in the back seat. He pulled a large bottle of spring water out of the bag, uncapped it and poured it on the ground. Semyon looked at him quizzically. His face changed dramatically when he saw Ned grab his vodka bottle and pour most of it into the water bottle. Semyon smacked him on the back and thanked him, calling him "buddy."

It was smart, he thought to himself, to reduce the risk of getting caught by the cops, and to keep Semyon happy and talking. Ned had seen him pout and sulk for long periods when deprived of what he wanted (which was usually vodka), and wanted him to provide more information about his new associates.

Back on I-95, Semyon was taking lusty swigs from his water bottle and chewing on some of the beef jerky Ned had bought him. Then he started up the conversation again without being asked. "Ah, Roman's okay," he said. "He's just careful is all."

Ned just nodded. Then when he realized Semyon would not continue without any prodding, he asked, "So, Roman is like Grigori? He gets his money from his factories?"

Semyon erupted into gales of laughter. "Grigori makes nothing from those factories these days!" he shouted. "Do you think those stupid Romanians and Bulgarians can keep up with millions of Chinese who will do the same work for a few grains of rice or to stay out of a prison camp? No, his factories make tiny amounts of money, but they give Grigori and his brothers legitimate companies—and it keeps the workers happy, so there are no more revolutions." He started laughing again, and when he stopped he sounded deadly serious. "No, Grigori makes his money other ways," he said. "Roman, too—just much more. It's all import/export—import money and export . . . whatever."

"Whatever?"

Semyon took a very long and serious look at Ned. Then he started laughing again. "Why are you being like this? You already know about the heroin in the coils. You are part of it."

"I put that together, but it kind of freaks me out a bit. Does anyone even do heroin anymore? Isn't it, like, something from the sixties or seventies?" Ned sincerely believed that; his experience trafficking drugs with the Sons of Satan had convinced him that pretty well everybody of a certain age smoked marijuana or hashish, but there was little profit in it; the real money was in cocaine and, to a lesser extent, methamphetamine, but the availability of crack had tended to erode those markets.

Semyon looked shocked. "Are you nuts?" he said. "Heroin users are everywhere. Their habit is evil. Always they come back for more, more, more."

"Really?"

"Yeah!" Semyon was quite adamant. "Hey, how much do you get for gram of coke?"

Ned had to do some quick calculations in his head. He had primarily been a distributer who passed coke from his bosses to dealers as a buffer against prosecution, but he knew Semyon was interested in the retail not wholesale price. Eventually, he said, "It depends on where you are and the purity of the product, but one hundred dollars if the market is good, sometimes less."

"Ha! Heroin is double that easy—and the market is always good," he shouted. "And since we get it from our people, we don't pay what you pay the Colombians and Mexicans for coke. The profit margin is huge—it makes selling coke look like selling goat meat on street corner." Ned accepted that simile as something of particular meaning to Semyon.

"Well, I like the sound of that," Ned said. "Is that how Roman got connected?"

Semyon shook his head. "He was not involved in heroin trafficking until the big guys started encouraging him," he said. "He made his big money in auto parts, but is better known for women."

"Women?"

"Yeah, women. You know—sell them?"

"Sell women? You mean like prostitution? He was a pimp?" He laughed.

"This is problem with Americans—the way the rest of the world works always has to be explained to them," said Semyon who was putting on his dopiest-looking face for added effect. "Not a pimp like you have here—some big black man with his stick and his 'hos.' No other country is as stupid about prostitution as America is. Even in places where it is officially illegal, it is always tolerated—except, for some reason, here."

"So if the cops are looking the other way, how does a guy like Roman make any money?" Ned asked with genuine curiosity. "Doesn't something have to be illegal for you to make any real money off it? I mean, you might pay twenty dollars for that bottle of vodka, but a sixteen-year-old kid would pay a hundred for the same bottle, right? That's how it works."

Semyon nodded and laughed. "But Roman is not a pimp, just like his boss is not some guy selling heroin on street corner. He is an *exporter*."

"He exports women?"

Semyon made a big deal about pretending to pray for patience with Ned's stupidity. "Yes, every country wants as many prostitutes as you can supply, but in countries with good economies—America, Germany, Sweden, Israel—only desperate women will do it, and nobody really wants them. And in many other countries—Turkey, Greece, Arab countries—the women are just too ugly, so everyone wants Eastern European girls. They are white, beautiful, poor . . . it's a perfect combination to make money."

Ned thought about what Semyon had said and thought back to his old girlfriend Daniela from Moldova. Although she refused to talk about it, Ned had come to believe that she had used prostitution as a way out of her native country. "Like Moldova?" he asked.

"Again with Moldova? What is it with you and that little asscrack of a country?"

Ned shrugged.

"But you are right, Moldova supplies a lot of girls," Semyon answered, the sheen of surprise still on his face. "Not the prettiest girls around, but they are plenty eager to work. Poorest country in all of Europe, you know, even worse than Albania!"

"I think I've heard how this works," Ned said. "A guy goes to small towns with a big car and fancy clothes and promises all the girls jobs as models and actresses in the West, but instead makes them strippers or prostitutes in America."

Semyon shook his head. "No, no, no, very few come to America. Someone tries it all the time thinking they get rich, but it doesn't really work," he said with a resigned shrug. "The girls learn English, run away, tell on their man. He goes to jail, they get a Green Card, maybe even citizenship through something called the witness detection program."

"Witness *protection* program."

Semyon smiled. "Yeah, in this country, you can tell on someone and the cops can take you away, give you a new name, a house, a job, even a Green Card, everything. It's crazy."

"So where do they go?"

"Who?"

"The women—instead of America, I mean."

"Oh, lots of places. The best method is to sell them to the Arabs who then sell them to Israelis, Turks, even Chinese," Semyon said. "They actually go to some pretty bad places. But they are always happy to get away from the Arabs. They are some really cruel guys, full of hate."

Ned changed the subject not just because he was thinking about his old girlfriend Daniela, but because he was approaching New York City. For someone who had never driven in a city with more traffic congestion than Wilmington, Delaware, and was piloting a gigantic SUV, it would take all of his attention just to stay out of serious trouble.

"Hey!" Semyon shouted. "Take the next exit."

"To the Goethals Bridge? Headed into Staten Island?"

"Yeah, I have someone I have to see," Semyon told Ned. "Drive to New Dorp. I'll guide you."

Within a few minutes, they arrived at a small storefront establishment called The Tube Bar. From the outside, it looked nondescript with just its sign out front and a neon "Budweiser" sign obscuring the only window. Inside, it was little better. Dusty and greasy at the same time, the bar was simple with just a few tables and chairs, a pool table, a jukebox and a waist-high bar. Ned chuckled to himself that it looked like Moe's from *The Simpsons*. There were a few haggard-looking customers inside, and an older, very large man behind the bar yelling threats into an old-style wired telephone.

He hung up by forcefully smashing the receiver down. As he turned to Semyon and Ned, Ned was surprised at how big and solid the old man looked. He must have been a former boxer or wrestler, Ned thought to himself. He had a ruddy face twisted by years of anger, closely cropped gray hair with a few red patches and he was covered in Navy-style tattoos.

"I don't need your bullshit right now, Simon," the old man shouted in what Ned thought was an almost impossibly scratchy voice. "Don't need it at all." There was some murmuring from the bar's patrons, and a few stabs of laughter.

Semyon approached the old man, who had come out from behind the bar to confront him. Although he was well within the angry old man's punch radius, he didn't flinch. In fact, he had that same droopy disinterested face he always had on when he wasn't giggling. The older man was raging and pacing around in front of Semyon, but all Semyon did was look at him.

"Well then, Red," he said quietly, "it would appear we have a problem."

Most of the bar patrons had gotten out of their seats and surrounded the two interlopers by this point. Ned was not smaller than all of them, just most of them. They were muttering.

"Really?" Red said threateningly. "Fuck off."

Semyon grinned broadly. "Red, my friend, you have me all wrong," he said with a lightness and confidence that shocked Ned. "Red, Red, Red, you treat me like I'm a bad man, like I am the enemy, but I am actually your best friend in the entire world. And I can prove it."

One of Red's tiny eyes opened wider as he lifted its eyebrow. "Oh, yeah? How?"

Semyon grinned again, then looked Red in the eyes. "Our mutual friend had told Vasilly to come and sort out your little problem," Semyon said slowly, putting extra emphasis on the name Vasilly. "I decided that since I was in the neighborhood, I could save him a trip. But if we can't work something out, maybe Vasilly will come and you can deal with him."

Red's face drained of color within a second, and Ned actually saw a glaze of perspiration form on his forehead before he could even react. Red stammered a little and then said: "Lemme get you a vodka, Simon, and what's your friend want? On the house."

Semyon thanked him, and Ned declined politely. After pouring the vodka, he went into the back room.

Semyon sniffed the vodka and poured it on the floor. "Cheap shit," he said. The bar's other patrons sullenly returned to their seats.

Red returned with a paper shopping bag that had been rolled up at the top. He handed it to Semyon, who thanked him. "There is a little something extra in there for you too," said Red.

"So kind," Semyon said. "But it had better not be more of this shitty vodka or Vasilly can come down here and do his own work."

Back in the car, Ned asked why Red was so scared of Vasilly.

"You don't want to know," Semyon answered with a laugh. Then his face turned serious. "But promise me you will not cross him . . . Promise!"

"Okay, okay," Ned returned. "I won't piss off Vasilly."

"Smartest thing I have ever heard you say."

* * *

Most of Brooklyn looked very much like Ned thought it would. First he saw graffiti-covered factories and warehouses, then a transition into tree-lined streets of closely packed row houses with cafés and trendy shops which, in turn, opened up into neighborhoods full of detached homes with fenced-in yards augmented by low-rise apartment buildings.

But Brighton Beach was something of a shock. Once Ned had passed under the elevated train tracks and into the neighborhood, he was surprised at how densely packed it was. All of the businesses and buildings—especially those under or in the shadow of the tracks—seemed to have been miniaturized. The streets were positively alive with traffic, and Ned had never seen so many people on the streets outside of a movie. The entire place was alive with all kinds of movement, both motorized and human.

But what really got to Ned were the signs. He'd seen some stores with Spanish signs in Wilmington, but every store here had its signs in Russian, complete with 3s and backwards Rs.

Semyon managed to stay sound asleep until Ned took a particularly sharp turn off Brighton Beach Avenue, jarring him. When they reached Brightwater Cresent, they came upon a huge public parking lot. Ned could see the ocean through his windshield.

"Park here!" Semyon barked.

"What?" Ned answered. "The GPS says it's three blocks from here."

"Yeah, but you could spend your whole life looking for parking in this neighborhood," Semyon said. "And it is tiny little New York blocks, not like what you have in Texas."

"Arizona," Ned said, lying.

"Same thing."

When they got out of the SUV, Ned felt the refreshing salt breeze. The beach looked a lot like the ones he knew from Delaware and Maryland, but the waves were much smaller and the water had a darker, greener color, unlike the steel-blue Atlantic he knew from farther south.

To Ned's surprise, Semyon walked towards the beach. "I thought it was on Brightwater," Ned said, running to catch up with him.

"That's just the mailing address, the front door is on the boardwalk."

The boardwalk was nice and breezy and, as they walked down it just a short way, Ned could see a transition between a heavily Hispanic east side to an almost uniformly white west side. They passed some nice little restaurants with names like Tatiana's and New Odessa and Ned was surprised to see most of them advertising fresh sushi. They kept walking until they got to a patio for a restaurant called Café Whatever. It had a hand painted sign and a busy patio.

As soon as he showed up, about half the crowd (Ned identified them as likely to be the bar's "regulars") greeted Semyon like an old friend. It took a few moments for Ned to recognize that they were all men. They all had dark hair and skin tones ranging from that of a blank page of photocopy paper to moderately tanned. They were all very hairy with thick eyebrows, and a few of the shirtless ones could be seen to be covered in tattoos. All were bedecked in far more gold than even the most vainglorious hip-hop artist would find tasteful.

They were all patting Semyon on the back or shaking his hand or at least waving. There was much conversation, and then someone in the crowd pointed to a table in the corner. Alone at it was a fat, red-faced man of about fifty. He was wearing nothing but swim trunks and a thick gold chain, and his upper body was covered in a series of intricate, but crudely drawn tattoos. He was passed out in his chair, with his chin buried in his fat neck. One of Semyon's friends—a big man who looked to be some sort of a leader or at least a favorite—said something in Russian to a pretty, thin waitress. Without any obvious acknowledgment of what the man said, the waitress picked up a can of Sprite from the outdoor section of the bar, brought it over to the sleeping man, opened it and rather dramatically poured it all over him. He sputtered for a moment, punched feebly into the air a couple of times, but never really woke up and, in fact, started snoring the moment he regained his comfort zone. The crowd started laughing uproariously.

As the laughter died down, the man who seemed to be in charge smiled at Ned and offered his beefy hand to him. "You must be our new friend, McGyver."

Ned chuckled. "It's Macnair," he said, shaking the man's hand firmly. "And you must be Roman."

The man looked shocked. His eyes widened so much that his entire irises were visible. "No, no, no," he said. "I am not Roman, I am his friend, Aleksei." Then he said something to the crowd in Russian—although Ned could make out the word "Roman," and everybody laughed. Aleksei then looked back at Ned smiling and invited him and Semyon inside. "First we eat, have a little relax," he said. "Then we do business."

It was darker inside and it took a moment for Ned's eyes to adjust. The bar had the same furniture inside as out and the walls were adorned with posters for all kinds of events Ned could not figure out. There was a small stage beside the bar, and a teenaged boy with a sloppy haircut and droopy wire-framed glasses was playing Lady Gaga songs on a Yamaha keyboard. He was dressed in a black suit with a pizza-patterned tie. Ned noticed that he had a cigarette in his mouth and beside him was a very full ashtray.

They got to a centrally located table that had two tough-looking guys at it. When Semyon got to them, he tilted his head quickly and made a clicking noise with his mouth. The two guys shot Aleksei a quick look. He did not acknowledge them and they grabbed their drinks and a half-eaten bowl of soup and left for the patio.

Since it was Ned's first time in a Russian place, Semyon ordered for him. Before long, he was given a bowl of red soup with a big dollop of sour cream in the middle, a plate of boiled dumplings with some kind of ground meat in them smothered in fried onions and a beer. Semyon and Aleksei both had big plates of what Ned guessed was sushi even though it looked more like simple chunks of raw fish than the intricate, rice-filled rolls he associated with the word. They both had large tumblers of what Ned guessed was vodka, although Aleksei's was red, almost like wine.

Ned complimented the meal, which he genuinely enjoyed. He asked Semyon what it was called and he told him something that sounded like "ber-nyeh-nyeh." Ned repeated it, as best he could. Semyon smiled and corrected him, but this time the word sounded more like "bru-nummy." Ned tried that. Frustrated, Semyon pulled a pen from his pocket and wrote "pelmeni" on a napkin. Ned laughed.

They were talking and laughing about Semyon's annoying habits when Aleksei shouted: "Enough! Time to relax!" He stood up. As though signaled, so did about a half-dozen other men, including Semyon. Those who had shirts on took them off. A different (older and heavier) waitress walked up to all of them with a basket into which the men put their cell phones, watches and wallets. Semyon signaled for Ned to follow suit. Some of the men finished their vodka before stepping outside. They all followed Aleksei off the patio, across the boardwalk and into the Atlantic Ocean. It was cold at first, but Ned didn't dare hesitate, although he did keep his pants on.

Chest deep in the water, surrounded by big, tattooed Russians, Ned felt like an idiot. Then Aleksei turned around, looked at him, took the cigar out of his mouth, smiled and said, "This is good, Macnair. We don't have to bother Roman."

Chapter Eight

Ned had never been in such a fancy restaurant in all his
life. Everything was red velvet, dark mahogany, crystal, sil-
ver or gold. The waiters wore uniforms with cropped red
jackets and black bow ties. Aleksei had led his group to a
big round table that already had four women at it. They
were all tall and rail thin with hair dyed a dirty blond and
all in their early twenties. They stood when Aleksei and
his group arrived and then arranged themselves in a boy-
girl, boy-girl mode with Aleksei, Ned and two others. The
remaining men went to another nearby table.

Aleksei beamed at Ned. "I will order for the table,"
he announced pompously then said something brief to
the waiter in Russian, who nodded and hurried away.

The girl to Ned's left leaned in and whispered breathily into his ear. "I am Petra, I am a model." Ned noticed that her accent was probably the thickest of all the people he had met so far. He took out his hand to shake hers, and withdrew it when he saw the look on her face.

"I'm . . ." he began, but she put her long-nailed fingers over his lips.

"We all know who you are. You are motorcycle man from America," and she imitated turning the accelerator on a huge pair of imaginary handlebars and made *vroom-vroom* noises with her mouth. The other girls laughed. "But you do not look like motorcycle man. Where is your beard, your long hair and your big belly?" She sounded almost disappointed that Ned looked like any mundane young American.

Ned couldn't help but chuckle a bit. "Yeah, some of the old guys look like that," he said. "But most of them look like me now . . . good for business."

Petra smiled and winked. "After dinner you must come to the Frying Pan with us," she said.

"What's the Frying Pan?"

"A nightclub with dancing on a boat," Petra smiled. "You will love it." She had a hard, cynical look about her and, though Ned was convinced that her only interest in him was professional, he couldn't help liking her anyway. Good looks aside, she also looked like she liked to have fun.

Aleksei interrupted. "Tonight, Macnair, you will have real Russian food," he said boastfully. "Not the goats' heads and dog meat that idiot Uzbek has most likely been giving you." He motioned to Semyon who was happily telling stories at the secondary table full of men. Ned couldn't help but think that they had been separated on purpose.

Although most of the night's conversation was in Russian—or whispered between the girls—Ned had a good time. He learned that Roman lived in a big house on Long Island near the beach and only came into the city when it was absolutely necessary. Aleksei said it was because he had everything he wanted out there, but Ned suspected there also might be dangers lurking in the city for such a man. Roman trusted Aleksei to handle things in his absence and his word was as good as truth to him.

Unlike many of the Russians—and Semyon—Ned had been careful not to drink too much. He was looking forward to going to the Frying Pan with Petra and her friends and told Aleksei as much.

Aleksei smiled widely, revealing a gold tooth. "I thought you would say that—she is very sexy," he said. "But there is one little, tiny roadblock in that plan." He saw the expression on Ned's face drop. "Aw, don't worry, you can go see Petra on that leaky old tub," he said. "But you just have to do one little tiny job first—Maxim and Artur will go with you—and then you have plenty of time to dance with Petra."

Maxim and Artur, the two other men at the table, laughed. Maxim was short and stout and had that round-faced Russian look Ned was becoming used to, while Artur was maybe six-foot-four with high cheekbones, blond hair and blue eyes. They laughed at what Aleksei said and nodded almost in unison at Ned. "Don't worry, they know what to do," Aleksei said. "They will help you, make sure you do the right thing."

Artur and Maxim escorted Ned outside where there was a black Lincoln and driver waiting for them out in front of the restaurant. They drove out of Manhattan over a bridge. On the ride, he learned that Maxim was from Rostov-on-Don, a big city in Southern Russia he said was warmer in the winter than New York. He had worked in a fish cannery until it closed down, so he moved to Moscow to earn his fortune. One thing led to another and now he was living, as he called it, "a nice life" in Queens. Artur said that he was from Estonia—which he pointed out in a boastful voice was closer to Sweden than it was to Moscow. His dad had been a police lieutenant before Estonian independence from the Soviet Union, and was considered by many of their neighbors a collaborator and an enemy of the new state. They emigrated to Moscow where his father struggled to find a decent job, and worked at a supermarket delicatessen until he died of a stroke. Artur, it seemed, had done no work other than being a gangster. Ned told them the story he knew they expected to hear.

They had driven out of New York City for quite some distance and Ned saw exit signs for suburbs with names like New Rochelle, Mount Vernon and White Plains. They finally turned into a nice-looking little town called Cortlandt Manor. The driver pulled up in front of a gated entrance and spoke to the men in the backseat in Russian.

They thanked him and exited the vehicle. Ned noticed that Artur had brought a large bag, suitable for hockey equipment perhaps, along with him. He looked at the intercom system on the gate and sneered. "Cheap piece of shit," he told Ned as he tore the cover off. He took some snippers out of his bag, cut a couple of wires and reconnected them. A section of the wrought-iron gate swung inwards under its own weight. Its creaking sounded very loud in the otherwise quiet night. "Come on," Artur said.

They stayed low as they approached the house. Ned could see flickers in the front window that indicated someone was watching television. He was surprised when he saw Artur and Maxim avoid the house entirely and run around the back. Maxim motioned to a smaller building at the back of the property. In the moonlight, Ned thought it looked like a garage or maybe a stable, but he could not be sure.

At the front of the small brick building were two big swinging doors meant for something large like a car, or a boat or horses. Off to one side was a smaller door, typical of a house, but wooden and windowless. Much to Ned's surprise, Maxim pounded on it. There was no response. He pounded again. From inside, Ned could hear an annoyed "yeah, yeah, yeah." About a minute or so later a boy of about eighteen, wearing nothing but a t-shirt and briefs, answered the door. He looked stoned and sleepy and took a moment to realize the men at the door were not the people whom he expected them to be. He let out a tiny squeak of a scream before Artur held a gun to his throat. Artur said something to Maxim who was searching in his bag. First he handcuffed the boy and then he put a big piece of duct tape over his mouth. He grabbed the boy by the back of his t-shirt and then frog-marched him to the big house's back door.

"Get us in," Artur demanded, his gun now at the boy's temple.

The boy cried and moaned, shaking his head. Maxim took a small, folding knife out of his jacket pocket. The boy's eyes got very large and Ned could hear his muffled screams from under the duct tape. He struggled and managed to break free from Artur's grasp, but skidded in the wet grass and fell down. As he was unsuccessfully trying to get up without the use of his arms, Artur turned to Ned. "Bring him back," he ordered. Ned could see that Artur's gun had swung around in such a way that it was pointed at him. Artur hadn't done it in a threatening manner, but a shot would have hit Ned if he had squeezed the trigger.

Ned approached the boy, trying not to look in his desperate eyes, and lifted him by the handcuffs. Apparently resigned to his fate, the boy stopped struggling. They rejoined the other two. Artur repeated his order to get them in the house. The kid nodded. Artur took the duct tape off. The boy approached a window that had been open just a slit and yelled into it. "Ma, Sarah, it's me. Lemme in . . . please!" The boy obediently tried not to sound desperate.

Before long, Ned could see a small figure appear behind the stained-glass window. Then he heard a couple of locks disengage. The door swung open inwards and a tiny, dark-haired perhaps Japanese woman started yelling. "Jake, I told you not to . . ."

She was interrupted by Maxim and Artur who bullrushed her out of the way and onto the floor. She was screaming and kicking until she saw Ned bring Jake inside and shut the door behind him. There was a look of wide-eyed horror on her face. "Jake, I told you getting mixed up with the drugs was a dangerous thing," she said while looking down and shaking her head. "So, do you think they're your buddies now? Are they great guys? Huh?"

Artur said something in Russian to Maxim and he laughed. "We are not drug buddies," Maxim told the sobbing woman. "We are business associates of your husband. Where is he, may I ask?"

The woman composed herself. "He's out, he's at the . . ."

At that moment a balding man with glasses entered the room. "Jesus Christ! What's all the . . . " He fell silent when he saw what was going on. He gathered up his wife and held onto her. "I don't know what you people want, but . . ."

"Yes you do, Mr. Weathers," said Artur.

"What my friend means to say is that we'd like to know if you have reconsidered Roman's business opportunity," Maxim said.

"What? No, I told your boss, I couldn't. It's totally illegal. In the wrongs hands, it could . . . and the feds would have my ass in a minute."

"That's too bad," Maxim shrugged, looked over at

Artur and nodded. Artur handed his gun to Maxim. Then he approached Jake—who was standing in the middle of the massive kitchen, still held by Ned. Artur steadied the boy with his left hand, and fished something from his jacket pocket. Ned saw a flash and then a spout of blood cascading from the boy's head. He immediately fell to the ground and turned involuntarily in pain. He was screaming and bleeding.

His mother rushed to his aid, screaming even louder.

The boy's father looked horrified, and said, "You cut his fucking ear off! You cut my boy's ear off!"

Artur grinned and held up a chunk of grayish-white skin. "Not all of it," he said. The father lunged at him, but stopped when he saw Maxim aim Artur's gun at his wife's head. Instead the man grabbed a towel and held it against his boy's head. He held his screaming family in his arms as the stream of blood from his son's mutilated ear finally began to ebb under the pressure of the towel. He swallowed. "Okay, okay," he said without looking up. "I'll see what we can do."

"There!" Maxim said, as though they were old friends talking about a fishing trip. "Was that so hard? Why do Americans always complicate everything?"

The woman stopped screaming and held her boy. The father stood up and looked at Maxim with utter contempt.

Maxim, whose facial expression did not change at all during the entire incident, looked at the man with an otherworldly calm. "You'll do more than 'see what you can do,'" he said. "You will get Roman what he needs. Because we also know that you have a young daughter—hiding in the house right now, I think—who you like enough not to banish to . . . how do you say it in English again? . . . horse house."

"Stable," Artur offered.

"Yes, she lives in here with people," Maxim said. "And I hate to sound like movie gangster here, but it would be a terrible shame if something were to happen to her." He said the last bit while rolling his hands dramatically and delivering the line as though he was embarrassed to even say it. "Besides, we are nice people. This one here is even American." Maxim gestured at Ned. "You don't want me to have to turn this matter over to Vasilly, do you?"

The man, already terrified, lost even more color. "Vasilly. Vasilly is real?"

Maxim smiled and nodded.

"I'll call Roman's man tomorrow."

"I thought you would," Maxim said. "But there's just one little problem." The room fell silent as Maxim turned towards Ned, who had been doing nothing but standing and watching since the boy collapsed out of his grasp. "Our new associate . . . no, our friend . . . he is our friend," Maxim said with what Ned thought was implied warmness. "He is new and we need to know we can trust him. So . . . how do I put this delicately? . . . he's going to have to hurt either your son or your wife."

"What?"

"You heard me. Choose."

"Do it to me."

Maxim made a disappointed noise with his tongue and teeth. "I'm sorry, I can't do that. It would be pointless. Choose between the two. Or maybe we should involve Sarah?"

The father didn't hesitate. He looked down and said, "My wife."

The woman screamed and tried to run, but Artur caught her. He pinned her arms behind her back. Maxim sidled over, his gun still aimed at the father's face. He handed Ned his knife. The woman looked at Ned, staring deeply into his eyes. The look on her face was of pure hatred. It was clear she expected no mercy.

Maxim broke the silence. "Stick it in her nose. Farther," he said dispassionately. "Now pull."

Ned did exactly as he was instructed. The woman doubled over and then fell to the floor, holding her gushing nose and emitting a shocking scream. Weathers rushed over to her with a towel and held it to her face.

She slapped him and crawled away, pressing the towel to her nose.

Ned looked up at Maxim. He could tell his own mouth was open, but could not shut it. "There!" Maxim said, patting Ned on the back. "Now we go."

* * *

Back in the Lincoln, Artur and Maxim were chattering happily to each other and Ned in Russian and English. Eventually, Artur broke the revelry. "Now we can go to the Frying Pan," he said jubilantly. "Except you have to change your shirt."

Ned looked down to the right side of his chest. The blood stains on his shirt were already turning dark brown on the white-and-blue pattern. It was only then when he realized that the cold, almost damp feeling of shock was still over him. "Don't worry," Artur said, before Ned could collect himself. "We can take you to Maxim's."

Maxim cut him short. "Uh uh, my wife sees him, she'll start asking questions and make me stay home with her—and I want to go to the Frying Pan."

Artur laughed and grabbed his cell phone. He hit a contact and then started talking in Russian, it sounded like he was negotiating in a jolly way. "Okay, we're going to Sergei's," he said to Maxim, then he looked at

Ned. "Too bad for you, though. Sergei won't have anything nice for you to wear." Then he gave the driver some directions in Russian.

They arrived not long after at a modest house in Queens. Ned saw some cars out front, but none he recognized. He was led in by Artur and Maxim, and the trio was greeted by a fat man Ned remembered from Café Whatever. They were led into a predictably garish living room and given vodkas. There were already four men present, and Ned was relieved to see that Semyon was among them. Although Semyon suddenly became very quiet and looked nervous when he saw Ned's face.

Artur began to recount the night's activities excitedly in Russian, re-enacting some of the more violent parts. Ned shuddered (he hoped imperceptibly) when Artur got to the part about him slicing through the woman's nose. At that point, Semyon rose from his chair, grinned proudly and put his arm around Ned. He made a loud pronouncement in Russian, and everybody except Ned laughed affably. Ned quietly asked Semyon if he could talk with him alone. Semyon reluctantly agreed.

"I can't go to the Frying Pan."

"Why not? Petra will be there."

"I know, I know, I'm just too freaked out."

"Why?"

"Didn't you hear? We just came back from torturing an innocent family?"

"Innocent? That man was innocent just because he is white American like you?"

"Well, his wife and son aren't gangsters."

Semyon shook his head. "That is no matter of ours."

"What about those people? They saw our faces. I think Maxim even called Artur by name once."

Semyon laughed. "These are not the kind of people who will call the police," he said. "And did Maxim mention Vasilly?"

Ned was shocked. "Yeah, yeah he did."

Semyon sighed. "There will be no trouble."

Ned put on a look he hoped Semyon would find significant. "Why?" he asked. "You're going to have to tell me why Vasilly holds such power over people."

"Another time," he said smiling. "But now, we party. You don't want them to think you aren't man enough to party, do you?"

"No."

Chapter Nine

Ned's eyes popped open with what he thought was an audible crack. Moving his dry eyelids over his eyes literally hurt, almost as much as the sunlight pouring in through the window. He started to get up to close the blinds, but came crashing back down. His head felt like it weighed a ton. It hurt to move anything, but when he moved his head, he felt a nauseous jolt in his gut.

Flat on his back, he rotated his head painfully left and then excruciatingly right. He was alone in a moderately sized bedroom, decorated in what he had come to recognize as the standard Russian style of warring patterns and over-vibrant solids. The door to the room was closed, as was the closet, but another was open. When he saw a toilet inside, he felt a wave of relief cross his body. Summoning all his strength, he ran for it.

He emerged about a half hour later feeling about twenty pounds lighter, but only very slightly relieved. He was walking stooped over with tiny, shuffling steps like a very old man. He made for the door and down the stairs. He recognized it as Sergei's house. He could hear talking from the kitchen.

When he entered, there was a loud whoop of approval from the three men sitting at the kitchen table. The pain that rushed through Ned's head was so immediate and intense, it was all he could do not to vomit right where he was standing.

Semyon must have realized that because, with a dramatic and condescending "awwww," he helped Ned to a chair. The Russians laughed. "There is only one cure," he said amiably and handed Ned a shot of vodka.

It was all he could do to get the vodka down, but once the burning, sick sensation went away, Ned had to admit he was already feeling a bit better. When he finally got up the energy to talk, he croaked, "What was that shit I was drinking last night?"

All the men laughed. "Cherry vodka," Semyon finally said. "It's an old Russian tradition. They fill a big vat with cherries or some other fruit (mangoes are also nice), fill it to top with vodka, then let it sit. After a while, the drink comes out red, tastes just like juice or soda, only better. It is very, very easy to get extremely drunk on it as it seems like you aren't drinking at all, until you try to stand up. I should have warned you—the hangovers can be absolutely brutal."

Ned shot him a dirty look that was so exaggerated that he hoped Semyon understood he meant it in a friendly way.

Sergei laughed. "It looked like he had a very good time with Nicky." Semyon was quick to agree, and gave Ned a playful cuff to the arm.

"Who's Nicky?" Ned asked. "I thought I was with Petra."

"You *were* with Petra," Sergei laughed. "But you did or said something I didn't catch, and she got very angry and called you 'a dirty drunk.'"

"Oh, yeah?" Ned said. "Then she left?"

"Not right away," Semyon added. "But after you said 'shut up, whore—go back to Moldova,' she did." He and Sergei laughed. Ned didn't remember a second of it. "We thought it was funny because she is very proud of being from Odessa. What an insult. I don't know how you do it."

"And Nicky?"

"Nikita, she is another model, also from Odessa," Sergei said. "She has always hated Petra, so when you insulted her, you immediately became Nicky's very good friend."

They all laughed, even Ned, who decided that the vodka-to-kill-a-hangover theory had significant merit. "But you of all people should know this," Semyon added. "You spent almost an hour in the ladies' room with her."

Ned was shocked at that news, but didn't want to sound like he didn't remember what happened, so he just nodded, and, when he thought of it, said, "We didn't talk much." Hoots of congratulation followed, and at least two guys patted Ned on the back.

* * *

Back in the SUV and headed towards Delaware, Ned realized not only that his hangover was fast disappearing, but that Semyon was still a little drunk. He was sipping vodka from his water bottle. Ned thought it was a good time to get a little more information out of him.

"How did you meet Vasilly?" he asked.

"In the army," Semyon said, and Ned was surprised that he didn't even pretend to protest the question. "We were both in the penal battalion in Chechnya."

"Penal?"

"Yeah, if you are in the army and you do something wrong, you get thrown into the penal battalion. They make you do the worst, shittiest jobs," he continued. "But it beats being shot at." He laughed a little.

Ned smiled. "What did you do to get in?"

"I didn't want to be in the army at all," Semyon said, clearly desiring to tell the story his way. "I was eighteen, it was 1995. I was caught stealing a BMW and they said it was prison or Chechnya for me. I chose prison. They sent me to Chechnya." Ned laughed. "Don't laugh, it is the worst place in the world—not something an American could ever understand in a million years," Semyon looked serious now, his glassy eyes focusing on something imaginary in front of him. "You are always cold and wet, starving, covered in lice, working, working, working, the officers kick the shit out of you every day and you have no idea how you will die. You don't think of *when* you will die because you are sure you will, you just think about *how* you will die. And you pray all day you don't get caught by those bearded bastards. If they take you prisoner, they enjoy torturing you—cutting off your fingers, your eyelids, your balls, while they laugh and yell *Allahu ackbar!*" He shook his head dismissively. "Then they hang the bodies upside down and hide behind them; so for us to get them, we have to shoot at the dead bodies of our friends. Bad shit."

"So they make the penal battalion fight?"

"Sometimes, but I was in a regular communications company until I got caught with some weed," he said. "I wouldn't give it to my sergeant, so they took me and put me in penal battalion. Our job was to load dead bodies onto planes and helicopters for transport back to Russia."

"And that's when you met Vasilly?"

"Well, I actually knew who he was earlier," Semyon said. "A bunch of different units had taken up residence in an old meat cannery, and he was a sniper for the infantry. Everybody knew him because he showed no fear and he hated the Chechens in a way none of us ever could."

"Why?"

Semyon sighed and looked over at Ned. Then he sucked in a deep breath and made himself comfortable for his little speech. "More history. When there was a Soviet Union, the bosses in Moscow made sure every republic, no matter how far or how awful, had a significant Russian population—anywhere from five to ten percent usually—just to keep an eye on the locals and to reinforce bonds."

Ned nodded. "That actually makes sense."

Semyon sniffed haughtily. "Vasilly's family were in Chechnya before the troubles," he said. "I forget what his dad did, but when the Soviet Union was falling apart,

Dudayev—a former Soviet fighter pilot who served in Afghanistan—declared an independent Chechnya with himself as president."

"So?"

"So? The place went crazy," Semyon shouted. "First thing Dudayev did was to let every prisoner out of jail— murderers, rapists, child molesters, everybody."

"Really? Did it get violent?"

"Yeah, like you wouldn't believe, but that's not even the worst part, at least for Vasilly," Semyon continued. "Chechen culture is not like ours or yours. Families there are organized into little clans called *tieps*. The *tieps* look after each other—if something happens to one member, the other members exact revenge. It keeps a lid on the violence."

"Really?"

Semyon wagged his finger at Ned's face. "Yes, but not for everyone," he said. "Russians have no *tieps*, they are just people, so they became sitting ducks for crime, they were subjected to robbery, rape, murder, kidnapping, enslavement—constantly—and they have no recourse, no help. That is why the war started."

"And Vasilly joined up to fight?"

Semyon looked down and made a noise that Ned thought he meant to be a laugh. "No, no, no, Vasilly's family was killed by Chechens when they robbed their apartment," he said. "And Vasilly dedicated his life to exacting revenge on every single member of the *tiep*—from what I hear, he killed twenty-six of those bastards, started with the children just to mess with their heads."

"And then he joined the army?"

"No, they came and got him," Semyon said. "Finished with the *tiep*, he was traveling to Moscow and was arrested on the train with illegal weapon."

"A gun?"

"No, a grenade launcher."

Ned's eyes widened. "So then he went into the penal battalion?"

"Nope, infantry."

"So how did he get put in the penal battalion?"

"At the cannery," Semyon said. "We had this small hole in the concrete fence through which we would trade with the Chechens."

"Really? You would actually trade with the enemy?"

"Yeah, of course," Semyon said. "But only with the kids, you know—five, six, seven, eight, nine—but once they got to ten years old, all they wanted to do was kill you."

"What did you trade?"

"We had things they wanted: bullets, grenades, flares, even generators," Semyon continued. "And they had things we wanted, like weed, butter, meat—you know."

"You would give the enemy ammunition to kill you?" Ned said, having a hard time wrapping his head around the concept.

"Sure, of course, it's what we had—and we were starving," he said vehemently. "They were starving too, but they would rather kill us than eat."

"So you and Vasilly got caught trading?"

"No, I got caught with a matchbox full of weed," Semyon said with a resigned tone, "but with Vasilly it was more complicated."

"How?"

"One night, he followed the kids back to their hideout, an old farm building about two kilometers from the cannery," Semyon continued. "He killed the boys and filled his pack and his pockets with all their stores—meat, canned fish, weed, pounds and pounds of it—then he took the boys and nailed them upside down by their feet to the outside of the house, took all the weapons and explosives out of the house and set them on fire."

"Why?"

"It made the Chechens think we were attacking," Semyon said, as though Ned was stupid for asking. "They came from miles and miles and miles to see their children hanging upside down, dead with their throats cut."

"What happened to Vasilly?"

"Oh, he went to the gate on the other side and gave each of the guards a can of condensed milk to get back inside. That shit is like gold over there," Semyon said. "Then he set up a store and started selling the stuff from the house back to us for rubles—real money."

"And he got in trouble for killing the kids?"

"No, some sergeant was trying to hit him in the jaw with the butt of his rifle."

"Why? Deal gone wrong?"

"How should I know? They don't need a reason. They beat us all the time. I once got a punctured lung because some captain didn't like my 'stupid Uzbek face.'" Semyon was angry now. "Anyway, Vasilly kicked him in the ribs and was taken away—ended up in my penal battalion."

Ned laughed. "Schlepping coffins?"

"Yeah," Semyon smiled again. "The Russian army always puts remains of the dead in coffins made out of zinc, then welds them shut. The official reason is that government thinks nobody should look inside. It's too sad, you know."

"It seems odd, with such a brutal war."

"It was, but none of us realized it," Semyon said with his index finger in the air, "until Pavel, Vasilly and I tried to move this one coffin—must have been six hundred pounds. Pavel figured that, since we are all starving, there was more than just a body inside. So we stole it, said it never arrived and took it to an old shed not far from the barracks. It took two weeks to open it, and inside we found . . ."

"Heroin."

"Yeah, that's right," Semyon smiled slyly. "Someone, someone high up, was smuggling heroin from Chechnya to Moscow in the coffins, getting rich while we starved and froze and broke our backs."

"And got shot at by Chechens," Ned added. "So what happened?"

"Pavel was killed. He was transferred out of penal battalion and back into a mortar crew. He was later found castrated with his fingers gone and his throat cut." Semyon sighed. "Vasilly was sent back to Moscow after the cease fire. He tried to sell the heroin himself, wound up with Mafia and was hired on as contract killer. He told them about me and when I returned to Moscow, I was given a job as a messenger and delivery boy. I owe Vasilly a great deal."

"Yeah, sounds like a great guy."

"He is, in his own way," Semyon said. "Just promise me you will never, ever do anything to make him mad at you."

Before Ned could answer, Semyon was snoring.

* * *

"You missed another day of work," Dave hissed into the phone.

"Yeah, yeah, yeah," Ned replied. "My *first* day missed at this job—and the Swede is cool with it."

"Don't call your boss 'the Swede;' show some respect," Dave shouted. "And I don't care if he's 'cool,' I'm some pissed off."

"Why, man?" Ned almost whined. "I was sick. Nobody cares but you."

"Really? Is that what you think? If I find out that you are up to something, I'll hand you over to the Sons myself, just for lying to me."

"C'mon, Dave."

"Yeah," he continued, sputtering with anger. "How'd you like to be Ned Aiken again? Good fuckin' luck. I'd give you fifteen minutes before I'd start checking the morgue."

"Relax, Dave. I just had a touch of strep and didn't want to infect anyone at work," Ned tried to sound beseeching. "I have a good thing here—why would I do anything to fuck it up?"

"I don't know why you assholes do anything you do; your logic got you into big trouble didn't it?"

"And it got me back out," Ned said. "Look, I learned my lesson. I want to stay at Hawkridge, want to do well. It's not like any other place where I've ever worked. They like me. They listen to me. I could even get promoted."

Dave laughed, Ned pictured his face softening. "Yeah, just stay outta trouble," he said. "Or you'll have even more trouble with me."

* * *

The next day in his office, Ned mused to himself that he wasn't really lying to Dave. He did enjoy himself there. And people there did like and respect him. He had great relationships with Katie and Juan, the other managers were cool and would sometimes have lunch or even go drinking with him, and even the Swede would pop by every couple of days with a few words of encouragement.

It was a pretty nice setup, and Ned didn't feel all that bad about not actually contributing to the company because, he rationalized, at least he wasn't hurting it.

The plan worked very much like he had been told it would. Steve, Hawkridge's manufacturing manager, would e-mail an order for cooling coils from the factory floor to Ned. He would then place an order for twice as many to Romania. They would arrive two weeks later, Ned would open them, and deliver the white-lettered ones to Steve, then ship the yellow-lettered ones to Detroit. It was all automatic, nobody ever questioned him.

And every two weeks or so, he'd get a visit from some college-aged kid who'd hand him an envelope that was marked "Macnair." It was small at first, just a couple of hundred bucks, but it began to grow. Ned started treating himself. Life was good. He was dressing better, living better, having a good time and—for the first time in a long time—looking forward to the future. Dave was quiet, the Swede appeared to be happy (as did his Russian friends) and he was making a lot of money. The Russians had even given him the surprise gift of a local "model" dropping by his apartment unannounced once. Ned was thinking strongly about getting a bigger place, definitely near the beach, somewhere where he could continue working on the old Indian.

There were a few snags, though. Chuck and Bob, the guys from the credit-assessment company mailroom, called him up a couple of times and insisted on a cut of his earnings. The first time it happened, he FedExed them four hundred dollars apiece. They called back and said he was insulting them. Ned argued that he hadn't made very much money yet, and that Grigori's people told him that he owed them nothing. When they called a third time, demanding payment in a threatening manner, Ned told them to take it up with Vasilly. After a long—and Ned assumed stunned—silence, Chuck began to sputter and swear and let out something in his own language that was both threatening and complicated. It sounded so much like something out of an old horror movie that Ned couldn't help but laugh. That enraged Chuck, who hung up.

Another thing bothered Ned. A number of the Ocean City Lawbreakers were busted in a drug raid—so many, in fact, that the Lawbreakers were moving members from other chapters to Ocean City to keep the chapter alive. Apparently, one of the Ocean City members or prospects had been working with the ATF. It was certain that he—and perhaps also someone looking to plea bargain—would tell the police that he had seen Jared Macnair, and that he had possible connections to the Russians. While it didn't weigh on him greatly, he did think about ways to distance himself from the Macnair identity.

He was actually doing that very thing when he received the third thing that bothered him these days—a phone call from a drunken Semyon. Ned honestly liked Semyon, but his calls were the worst. He'd drone on for hours about the most mundane things, complain about slights—many, Ned felt, were more imagined than real—and sometimes completely forget who he was talking to and start rambling on in Russian.

This time, though, Semyon sounded pretty well put together. He had clearly had a couple of sips of vodka, but he was unlikely to go off on one of his long and barely coherent soliloquies. Instead, he went straight to the point, at least by his standards.

"Did you like my present?" he asked.

"Which one?"

"What?" Semyon asked, angrily. "The girl!"

"Was that you?" Ned asked mockingly.

"Who else would buy you a date?" Semyon was beginning to realize he was being made fun of. "You have other such friends?"

"Hundreds," Ned said, laughing.

"Even I have to admit lots of people like you these days," Semyon said. "Your ability to do your job and stay quiet has been noticed."

"Really?"

"Yes, and you are due to get big reward."

Immediately, images of luxury cars popped into his head. "Oh yeah?" Ned said. "That's great—what am I getting?"

"An all-expenses-paid trip to Moscow with Grigori and me!"

Ned was shocked. The Cadillacs and BMWs in his head turned into cops and prison guards. "You know I can't go to Russia," he spat out. "My ID is good, but it's not good enough for an international flight. Do you want to see me in a federal penitentiary for fifteen years?" He knew that if he tried to get on an international flight with his Eric Steadman ID, he'd never get on the plane. Security would call Dave, he'd have his protection lifted and the Russians would then be racing with the Sons of Satan to kill him. And if he tried to use the ID the Russians had given him, who knows what would happen? Immediately and without warning, the idea entered his mind that the Russians had somehow found out that he was dealing with the FBI, and just wanted him to get into a car to kill him.

Semyon interrupted that thought with a loud sigh. "All you ever do is worry," he said. "Don't you think that we think of these things before we make them happen? Grigori does not want to lose such a valuable asset as you. Rest assured, your ID is good enough for where we are going to take you."

Their conversation was friendly after that, with Semyon explaining that Ned hadn't seen anything compared to what awaited him in Russia. Ned said that he was sure of that. After saying good-bye, Ned sat in front of the TV blindly switching channels, drank almost an entire bottle of Jim Beam and smoked two joints before he finally nodded off at just before three a.m.

Chapter Ten

It surprised Ned that they put Pyotr in the car with him rather than Semyon. They were in an old beige Ford Taurus that Grigori had parked in front of his headquarters in Detroit. The plan was that the group would travel over the Ambassador Bridge into Canada in separate cars and then meet at a bar in a little town called Tilbury, about forty-five minutes down Highway 401.

As they approached customs, Ned took out his Jared Macnair passport and Pyotr handed him his. The customs officer—a heavyset woman in her late twenties—looked them over disinterestedly. "Nationality?" she asked.

"Both American," Ned replied.

"Where do you live?"

"I'm in Grosse Pointe, and he's from Southfield."

"What's the purpose of your visit?"

"Visiting relatives. My sister married a Canadian guy and now they live in Newmarket."

"Newmarket?" She smiled. "I'm from Aurora."

"I'm sorry," Ned replied. "This is my first time in Canada. I only know Newmarket from a map and from my sister's description."

"Oh, well, here are your passports, Mr. Macnair and Mr. Taglietti. Have a nice trip."

"Tal-yetti," Pyotr corrected her pronunciation. Ned smiled at his pretense.

As they drove out of Windsor and into the countryside, Ned couldn't put the landscape and his vision of what Canada was like together. All his life, he'd been sold an image of Canada bursting with natural beauty—majestic mountains, rich, endless forests and crystal-clear water teeming with wildlife—but all he saw here were flat, almost uniform farms, clapboard bungalows, gas stations, convenience stores and maybe a muddy stream or two. It looked a lot like places he'd been to. And Pyotr didn't help break the boredom. Even though he had the best English skills of any of the Russians he had dealt with, he didn't have much to say. He felt no need to divulge anything about his own life and had made it clear he had no interest in Ned's. Ned found himself missing Semyon's nonstop prattle, and all he had were a steady supply of classic rock and country channels on the radio to keep him company.

They arrived at Tilbury and turned off to find the bar. When Ned saw four customized Harley-Davidsons and a pair of pickup trucks parked outside he knew who was waiting for them. He knew this area had been Outlaws territory for a very long time—which made sense because it was so close to the club's Detroit head-quarters—but after some mass arrests, the Bandidos took over. But then they had an internal war with a lot of deaths and basically vanished from the area. And now, Ned was unsurprised to learn, the Hells Angels were in charge.

Even though there was little contact (or love lost) between the Sons of Satan and the Hells Angels, the presence of *any* bikers made Ned nervous. He and Pyotr were the first of their group to arrive, and Ned suggested they wait outside for the others. Pyotr shot him a dirty look and told him that it was too hot outside and that he was hungry.

Inside the bar, Ned smelled cheap draft beer and stale cooking grease before he saw the group of men gathered around a couple of tables. They had been chatting, but fell silent when Ned and Pyotr walked in.

Without a second thought, Ned recognized them as bikers, but not as particularly important ones. All of them were white, some had shaved heads, a couple wore long beards and all of them had lots of tattoos, silver-colored jewelry and Harley-Davidson logos on their clothes.

The bikers scanned Pyotr and examined Ned carefully as they walked in. Bikers from other gangs were never safe in a room full of Hells Angels, especially if it looked like they were trying to make a drug deal in their territory. And considering whom he was traveling with, that could be an easily made assumption.

But then Ned remembered something. Although he had once been a prominent biker (and was passing for yet another), he didn't look like one anymore. His hair was closely cropped, but far from shaven. He had no facial hair, no visible tattoos and wore no jewelry aside from a modest watch. He was wearing a light-blue and yellow Hawkridge golf shirt and tan canvas pants. If anything, he mused to himself, he looked more like an undercover cop than a biker.

Pyotr was another matter altogether. Although his appearance raised no suspicion with the woman at customs, the trained eyes of the bikers saw more. Massive, he had a shaved head and one of those goatees fat guys grow to make their face look thinner. He was wearing a powder-blue and white track suit with a white t-shirt on underneath. Unzipped, it revealed a wealth of tattoos. And he was dripping in gold, although he had hidden most of it when he went over the border. With the jewelry back on, even a small child could guess he had something to do with the drug trade: He walked by the bikers without so much as a glance their way.

After Ned and Pyotr found a table at the other end of the room, the bikers started talking again, but in hushed tones. Ned couldn't make out what they were saying, but he knew they were almost certainly talking about them.

A few minutes passed before Grigori and a pair of his associates came in and sat with Ned and Pyotr. Like Ned, they were dressed casually and unremarkably. Grigori yelled something in Russian at Pyotr, and he looked hurt. Grigori ordered chicken wings and sodas for everyone at the table, he made it clear there was to be no drinking. About a half hour later, Semyon came in with two more men and joined them. They were dressed in much the same way as Ned and Grigori.

Semyon made an effort to sit beside Ned, but was rebuffed by Grigori. There was a great deal of discussion in Russian, and Ned waited to find out what was going to happen. Grigori gave Pyotr his car keys and the big man reluctantly went out into the parking lot. Semyon got up and stood beside Ned. He spoke into his ear, *sotto voce*, that the plan was for them to fly to Russia posing as a mixed government/corporate group heading to a conference about heating and cooling technologies in Moscow. Grigori, as vice-president in charge of technology for Premier Solutions, was leading the group. Vasilly was to be a Russian government advisor and the rest of them were engineers. Except for Ned. He was to pose as a grad student studying the differences between how the Russian and American manufacturing sectors were adapting to challenges from China and other low-wage countries. Grigori had made all the arrangements and had gotten the papers in order. And he was some pissed off with Pyotr for not dressing the way he told him to. He was going to have to go back to Detroit. Pyotr came back in, struggling with a pile of briefcases—all them different brands—and a single backpack, which he gave to Ned.

Semyon then instructed Ned to get in his car with Vasilly and Andrei, because Pyotr was going to take the Taurus back home. Ned hoped he hadn't seen the flicker of fear dance across his face. All Semyon did was smile.

The bikers, who up until this point had been quiet, approached Semyon as a unit when he went over to the bar to settle up the tab. Ned looked over his shoulder to watch and thought to himself that it was typical of biker behavior to approach the smallest of the group when he was alone. Pissed off, he got up and joined his friend. Just as he arrived, the oldest-looking biker asked Semyon, "What are guys, some kind of terrorist cell or something?"

Semyon smiled. "No, man, we are Russians, your enemy *before* the Arabs," he said jocularly. "We are all best friends now."

"So you're communists?" the biker snorted, and all his friends laughed in support.

"Trust me," Ned interjected. "These guys are the opposite of communists."

"Who asked you?"

At that, Vasilly got out of his seat, approached the group and gently pushed Semyon aside. He looked at the big biker in the eye and sneered. Vasilly came up to his chin. He let out a little chuckle. The biker glared at him. In one move, too quick for Ned's eyes to follow, he held a pistol to the biker's testicles and a knife just under his jawbone. Ned stepped back, Semyon just smiled.

"So you think you're a big man, just because you have a weapon?" the big biker asked Vasilly. As he was finishing his sentence, the whole bar heard one of the younger bikers cock a double-barreled shotgun. The bartender hit the ground instinctively, and the waitress ducked into the ladies' room.

Semyon laughed. "No, no, no, he is very *small* man," he said, clearly enjoying himself. "That is why he would have no problem killing you all—he has, as you say, 'issues.'"

"Shut up, you fuckin' commies," the biker with the shotgun said, trying to insult them and pointing the shotgun at Ned. "Back off, or your faggot friend here gets splattered all over the walls."

Vasilly, for the first time indicating he understood English, let out a derisive laugh.

Just as it looked like things were going to get very ugly, Grigori stood up. He faced the big biker with Vasilly and put his hand on his shoulder. "Don't worry about these boys, Zeke," he said warmly. "They don't know who they're talking to and they get a bit nervous sometimes." Then he and Zeke laughed.

"I know, I know. Put down the gun, shit-for-brains. These are 'comrades' of ours," Zeke commanded. The young biker did as he was told. Vasilly slowly followed suit. Zeke and Grigori went through a door with a sign that said "employees only" for a private conference. Ned noticed that both of them had briefcases. The bikers and Russians in the room watched each other uneasily.

After twenty minutes or so, the door opened and Grigori and Zeke came out, talking as friends. Grigori motioned for the Russians to leave. They did. Semyon and Andrei escorted Vasilly out first.

* * *

In the car—an old Lincoln—Semyon was driving, Ned was in the passenger seat while Vasilly sat in the back, reading beside Andrei. Andrei waited until they were out of town before he said, "Your friends, they are not so tough." Then he let out a little giggle.

"Those were not my friends," Ned replied. "If you'll remember, I was the one with a shotgun pointed at me."

Vasilly sniggered a bit from the back seat without lifting his eyes from the page he was reading. Semyon let out a genuine belly laugh. "That's true," he said. "The Sons of Satan no longer have much use for you."

"Those were not Sons of Satan."

"Who were they then?" Andrei asked mockingly. "Lawbreakers? Hells Angels? Outlaws? The Banditos?" His sarcasm escalated with each name he spit out.

"None of the above," Ned said. "They were a puppet gang, sort of like the minor leagues, for the Hells Angels."

"Minor leagues?"

"In sports in America, the minor leagues are where players go when they are not yet ready for the big leagues," Ned explained. "They learn, get better and have a chance to get rich."

"We have this in Russia too—for hockey and soccer," Andrei said, then muttered something to Vasilly, who did not acknowledge him, but lazily turned a page in his book. "How could you tell?"

"Their tattoos," Ned said. "They all had '81,' 'Support 81' or 'Big Red Machine' on them – that means they are a support gang for the Hells Angels, but are not allowed to have the actual words 'Hells Angels' on them."

"Why '81'?"

"'H' is the eighth letter of the—I mean our—alphabet and 'A' is the first."

"Our tattoos have meanings too," Andrei said. "But nothing so lame as that."

"Like what?"

"Real things based in our rich tradition, not crossword puzzles clues," Andrei continued. "A cat is for a thief, a skull means murder, different symbols mean different things. I had to laugh the other day when I saw young girl in the mall with a barbed-wire tattoo on her arm. In Russia, that means she is in prison for life." He laughed. "We have real artistry. You saw the cathedral on my back? And some tattoos are not what you would call voluntary. A prison slave may get crucifix. A child molester may get dagger over his heart."

"I like your 'rich tradition' of thieves and murderers and child molesters, and I have to admit that we have something similar in ours," offered Ned. "But we generally just sew patches onto our jackets for our accomplishments and affiliations."

"You hear that Vasilly? Here, if you kill a man, you get to sew a little piece of ribbon onto your blouse." Andrei now sounded disgusted with Ned. "We wear ours on our skin!"

"It's not like bikers are afraid to get tattoos—they get lots of them," Ned defended his culture. "But sometimes you don't want to advertise exactly who you are in prison. Say you are in a Bandidos block and you're a Hells Angel—there would be trouble."

"Ours are the opposite!" Andrei sounded stunned. "If I walk into prison in Russia, the Virgin Mary says I started as criminal when I was too young to decide on my own, the cat says I am thief, two skulls say I have killed two men. I *want* the other prisoners to know this. It's like a résumé. Besides, the quality of your tattoos shows how important you are. Mine are like fine art, Pyotr's are like cartoons."

"But what if a rival gang controls the prison?"

"It doesn't work that way in Russia," Semyon snorted. "Over there, criminals regard other criminals as fellow professionals—at least in prison. Your gang affiliation is not so important as your ethnic group."

"Really?"

"Yeah, our system works more like Italians used to. Rival groups tolerate each other unless there is a problem," he shrugged. "Then it gets solved."

"What was that you said about ethnic groups, though?"

"Well, there can be a problem if two specific nationalities are put together if they hate each other," Semyon said. "Like Armenians and Azerbaijans, that sort of thing. I'd really hate to see any Chechens in a jail with Vasilly—any Muslims actually. Hell, anyone with a beard." For the first time, Ned saw a tiny curl of what could have been a smile on Vasilly's lips.

For the rest of the ride, they spoke about the differences between Russian and American prisons and how, for many people from the former Soviet Union, life in an American prison represented an improvement over their lives back home. Before too long, they stopped at what appeared to be a Canadian military airfield. They were welcomed by two soldiers in fatigues at the gate, who took their names and then waved them through. They met up with Grigori and his men who were speaking with a Canadian captain in a green uniform. He welcomed them to his base and told them that their

flight would be ready "as soon as they checked the passports and visas."

Ned was paralyzed with fear until he saw that the
paperwork was being examined by hand by a pair of
disinterested privates. Then he grinned. A few moments
later, they were walked out to the tarmac where a giant, bulbous jet with Russian military markings and the
words "Atlant Soyuz" on the side was waiting. All of
the men shook hands with the Canadian officer as he
wished them a good trip.

The plane had two different classes inside, which
Ned surmised were for officers and enlisted men. His
group sat in the officer's area. They were all talking in
Russian, so Ned nodded off and went to sleep, as he always did in airplanes.

When he woke up, they were still in the air. There
was nothing below him but darkness. He had no idea
whether he was over the Atlantic Ocean or Europe. He
asked Semyon. Delighted that his friend was awake,
Semyon looked at his watch and told him they were
likely over Norway or Sweden, and that it would not be
long until they were in Russia.

A couple of the other guys had fallen asleep, and
Vasilly was staring at Ned. It was the first time since
he'd been sent to clear his identity with the Ocean City
Lawbreakers that Ned felt nervous about being with these

guys. Logic told him that they would not go to all this expense if they wanted to get rid of him, they'd just kill him in Wilmington or Detroit. If they were taking him to Russia, they must have bigger plans for him. And Grigori had asked the Swede to talk to Dave about the time off for a conference (although he said it was in Anaheim). But he still couldn't shake the feeling of unease. He'd been told that fear came from the unknown, but the more he knew about Vasilly, the more afraid he was.

But he couldn't dwell on it. Semyon wouldn't stop talking to him about Russian etiquette and table manners. He also tried to teach him a few conversational Russian phrases, but none of them stuck.

The entire group was awake now, and talking in Russian. Semyon was still chattering at Ned as they hit the tarmac. The giant plane landed in what appeared to be a commercial airport, but there were a few other military-looking planes and helicopters there as well. They waited calmly on the runway until the pilot and co-pilot came out of the cockpit to say good-bye. Ned did as the others did, getting up on cue and shuffling over to greet the crew. It surprised him (not to mention Semyon) to hear *do svidaniya* come out of his mouth. It was the first Russian he had ever spoken other than the halting and poorly received lesson Semyon had tried earlier in the plane. The pilots also looked stunned and took a moment to recover before laughing and patting Ned on the back.

Semyon told him that his accent was so thick that the words he said were barely recognizable, but that the pilots appreciated that he was trying. He added that other Russians would too.

As they walked down the staircase from the plane, Ned could see that there were three Hummers waiting for them right on the runway. And they were not military vehicles, but civilian models like you might see on the streets of Los Angeles. The lights of the airports revealed how thick and glossy their black paint was and the chrome touches gleamed. Each had a driver in a black suit who was standing beside the vehicle with the passenger door open. The Russians from the plane piled into the SUVs without acknowledging the drivers. Ned followed Semyon into the last one, with Evgeni.

"Where are we?" Ned asked.

"We're on our way to see Viktor," said Semyon. Evgeni just stared out the window.

"Is he the boss?"

"He's *a* boss," Semyon said. "You'll understand when we get there."

The powerful SUVs raced down well-paved but largely untraveled roads. Cruising at what Ned estimated at about eighty-five miles per hour, the three big trucks stayed in formation, often passing slower vehicles. Suddenly, the first swerved wildly into the oncoming lane, followed by the others. "What the hell was that?" asked Ned.

"Sometimes the locals will set traps or homemade roadblocks for luxury cars," Semyon said absentmindedly. "Rob people, steal car. That's how they do business."

"Fuckin' Uzbeks," added Evgeni in English. Semyon yelled a mad tirade at him in Russian. Evgeni snorted his disapproval and went back to looking out the window.

Semyon smiled at Ned. "Don't worry," he assured him. "We are the last people they want to stop." Then he reached into a compartment in his door and handed Ned a Sig Sauer handgun and pulled out what looked like an Uzi for himself. Evgeni protested something loudly in Russian. At first, Ned thought he was upset that Semyon had given him a gun, that the Russian still did not trust the American interloper. But then he saw Evgeni rummage dully through the compartment full of weapons until he came upon a sawed-off shotgun. He smiled, put it in his lap and went back to staring out the window.

Before long, the little convoy slowed and turned down a smaller gravel road. It was in heavy woods and so dense that Ned could no longer see any stars or the moon.

After about a half-mile they came upon a wrought-iron gate and a fieldstone wall that looked to be about twelve feet high. At the gate, there were two guards with AK-47s. One guard spoke with each driver while the other took up a firing stance. When the guard approached Ned's vehicle, Ned could see that he was short and stocky with a round face. Ned took him to be Korean. He spoke amicably with the driver for a moment or two, then had him roll down the rear window. He stuck his head into the back and looked directly at Ned with his AK-47 pointed at him. "Beng! Beng! I shoot you, cowboy!" he said to Ned. "Velcome to Russia, G.I. Joe."

Ned gave a little chuckle to show he wasn't scared. Semyon sighed. "Fuckin' Kyrgyz," he said. "They always think they are funny, but nobody else does."

The guards waved the convoy through. Ned noticed that the gravel changed to cobblestones once through the gate. They drove up a semicircular lane that was illuminated by a series of gaslights. They stopped beside a towering mansion whose size and grandeur Ned could have only imagined before he had seen it. As he stepped out of the car, he could hear the gushing of the many fountains that lined the driveway, as well as some men greeting the rest of his party. A peacock lazily strutted by as it investigated the commotion. Ned also heard what he thought could have been a lion or a tiger roar.

The group was moving inside. Semyon motioned for Ned to follow. When he came close, Semyon whispered, "Good thing you slept on the plane. These guys are going to stay up all night."

Chapter Eleven

The house was even more impressive inside than out. It was cavernous and decorated so lavishly that Ned considered it more of a castle than a residence. He was particularly impressed with the large fountains in the atrium.

But he didn't have long to stand gawking. Ned's party was escorted quickly through the atrium and down a long corridor. Rooms branched off it, lavishly decorated and painted in lurid colors. Ned took in the oil paintings, huge canvases with ornate frames, and realized they told some kind of heroic story, each featuring the same man, but each depicted him in a different role—barbarian, knight, commando. As the group made its

way out the back doors, Ned saw that there was a helicopter parked on a large paved area on the other side of a
large swimming pool. He surveyed the grounds. Despite
the darkness, he could make out the area around him as
a magnificent patio of sorts, almost like a piazza. Beyond
that, the grounds were dominated by rolling hills with
manicured lawns leading up to a densely wooded for-
est. There was a big, low-slung building that looked to
be a multi-car garage.

His group was greeted by two men in black suits
and matching ties. Ned couldn't keep his eyes off their
guns, which appeared to be gold-plated AK-47s. They
welcomed the group and led them to the helicopter.
Once they were seated and the engines began to rev up,
Ned asked Semyon, "Is all this Viktor's?"

"All this and a lot more," Semyon answered. "Wait
and see."

"Where are we going now?"

"Viktor's nightclub," Semyon answered. "It's just
outside Moscow."

"I thought we were just outside Moscow?"

"We are."

Semyon started talking with Evgeni, and Ned
looked out his window. He was shocked at how huge
Moscow was. It first showed up as an illuminated circle
far below them, but as the helicopter flew low over the

city, Ned was astounded by mile after mile of poured-concrete apartment blocks. He marveled at how many people—millions—lived in what appeared to be exactly the same building duplicated over and over for miles. As they turned northwest, the buildings began to spread out and trees and parks became more common. As the helicopter descended, Ned could see that they were at a small airport and there were, again, three Hummers with uniformed drivers parked close to where they landed.

Hustling off the helicopter and into the car, Ned noticed the drivers' exertions in opening and closing the doors of the Hummer. Semyon saw Ned staring, and said, "Bulletproof, blast-proof—you can't be too careful when you're Viktor, or friends of Viktor." Ned managed a smile.

They drove from the airfield through a suburb with a few apartment buildings and professional or government buildings. Ned thought he heard the distinctive *bud-bud-bud* of automatic weapon fire in the distance, but he couldn't be sure. As they drove, the area became more commercial, more Western-looking. Some even had signs in English.

Despite the thickness of the windows in the Hummer, Ned could hear the thumping of the Eurodisco even before he saw the building. It looked like it had been an old warehouse, but was now painted a lurid purple and covered in neon. Flashing above the entrance was a sign that said "Club MegaSexxxy."

There were two gargantuan men out front with AK-47s. Beside them was a lineup of young men in their best outfits, clearly hoping to get in the building. The drivers led Ned's group past the line—Ned could hear them grumbling and groaning—and up to the big men. They spoke with one another and laughed. One of the bouncers opened the metal door, releasing an almost deafening blast of music.

Inside, it was hot and barely lit. As they made their way through the crowd, Ned began to think that he'd never seen so many beautiful women in one place. Most of the other partiers seemed to be middle-aged men—some in suits, others in workout wear, all of them covered in gold. They were drinking and laughing and more than a few were smoking cigars. The dance floor, lit from below, was packed with young girls dancing, drinking and laughing.

Semyon snapped his fingers in front of Ned, who was clearly ogling the dancers. "Don't worry, man," he shouted. "You'll get your chance later. But we have work to do—after a drink."

The group collected around a table that had clearly been reserved for them. Ned was listening to a story of Andrei's about his own time in Chechnya, when he heard someone ask, "American?"

Ned swung his head around. The man who asked was dressed nicely but casually. He looked like he had a $200 haircut and an easy smile that revealed perfect teeth. Ned told him that he was American. The man smiled again and asked him to join him and his friends at his table. Ned looked over to Grigori, who nodded.

The man introduced himself as Damian Hewitt and told Ned he was from just north of Chicago. Ned followed him to a table with two other men. "This is Don, from Tallahassee," Damian said, pointing at a gray-haired man. "And this is Robin, he's a tea bag."

"Tea bag?"

"From England."

Ned shook their hands and the four of them talked about some of their experiences in Russia and with the Russians. Before long, they were laughing and having a good time. Ned found out that they were sales managers from a Seattle-based soda company and they were in the club trying to convince Viktor's people to allow them to distribute their product in Russia.

"So Viktor's going to sell your soda?"

"Nah, man," Robin said. "We already have a distributor set up. Viktor just has to okay it."

"Okay it?"

"Yeah. It's how business is done here. You know . . ."

"Not really."

"Well, what business are you in?" Don asked. "Why are you here?"

"I'm in HVAC. I just work for these guys."

"What's the scam then?" Robin asked.

"No scam, it's all legit," Ned said, and immediately wondered how convincing he sounded.

The three other men laughed. "They're keeping you in the dark then," Don said. "Every business here is a scam one way or another. It goes all the way to the top."

"You mean Viktor?"

The three men laughed again. "No, the top," Damian told him. "You know, Putin."

Ned was sincerely shocked. "What?"

"It's true. The big guy gets a cut of everything," Damian replied. "Nothing major happens in the whole country without his say-so."

"So you're telling me that the president is nothing more than the top gangster?"

Damian looked exasperated. "Do you remember when Putin stole Bob Kraft's Super Bowl ring?" he asked.

Ned did remember. "But he said it was all a mistake," he said. "That he thought it was a gift."

Damian laughed. "Did he give it back?" he asked.

Just then, Semyon approached and told Ned it was time for their meeting with Viktor. He then led Ned to a staircase at the back of the club. At the top was another thick metal door, almost like a vault's, guarded by two more armed men. Once behind it, Ned realized the massive din from the disco downstairs had been reduced to a low rumble. They continued to walk until they came to a huge room that was decorated in much the same style as Grigori's office back in Detroit. But there was no desk here, no office chair. Instead it was outfitted for comfort with many sofas and a large, red velvet bed.

At the back, two men stood engaged in conversation. One was in a magnificent crimson-and-gold chair, the other on a matching, but much less impressive couch. The big man in the throne-like seat—whom Ned recognized as the man in the oil paintings in Viktor's house—raised his thick eyebrows and looked over at them. The other man immediately jumped up and walked over to them. He was thin, with tight skin on his face. He was balding and had a very closely cropped mustache and round wire-frame glasses. Ned immediately thought he looked like a college professor.

The man greeted Grigori politely and then the other men. Saving Ned for last, he shook his hand and said, "Mr. Macnair, so good of you to come. Mr. Volchenkov will be so delighted to meet you."

He didn't look it. Viktor looked bored—as though he had been disturbed—and spoke only to Grigori. After a moment or so, he waved his big right hand around in the air. The guy in the glasses immediately stood up and motioned for everyone in the group except Grigori to join him. He then took them on a tour of the room, describing in both Russian and English some of the valuable works of art and historical artifacts Viktor possessed. One thing, in particular, caught Ned's attention—a pair of gold-plated handguns with diamond-studded grips. Ned knew some gun nuts back home in the States, but it seemed to him that the Russians fetishized guns. The man in the glasses was still talking when Grigori stood up and told his group they had to go.

They returned to the bar and Grigori took a large table over from a lesser group. Before long, girls started to arrive. Many of the girls crowded around Ned who was not just the youngest guy around, but also clearly not from the area. All of the girls tried their English out on him. One, in particular, named Nina, spoke good English and they struck up a long conversation.

* * *

The next morning, Ned woke up in a small but luxurious hotel room to see Nina combing her hair in front of a mirror. She saw him, smiled and told him she'd see him later. She gave him a gentle kiss on his forehead and left.

It all came flooding back to him. After dancing, eating and drinking at the club, his group had jumped into the Hummers and drove back to the airfield. Then they had taken the helicopter to Viktor's yacht, moored in the Moskva. The hotel room he was in was not a hotel room at all, but a ship's cabin. Ned could see the helicopter parked at the ship's stern.

He dressed and went outside. He could see that the ship was moored next to a few others of similar size and many smaller boats. He heard voices behind him, so he turned around and stepped down to a wooden deck. The rest of his group were sitting at a table while various models from the nightclub were sunning themselves on deck. Nina was with them, reading an English edition of *Harry Potter*.

Semyon called Ned over and offered him a seat. After he was seated, he noticed the waiter. Not sure if the waiter spoke English or not, Semyon ordered for Ned. Everybody seemed to be having a good time, and even Evgeni and Grigori were speaking English. Vasilly even once lowered his book and grinned while Semyon was parodying Evgeni's attempts to dance the night before.

After a breakfast of cold sausage, blinis, eggs and coffee, Grigori told the group in English that they had one more job to do before they were on their own to do whatever they pleased. They would enjoy the morning on the yacht, but would have to meet at the helicopter at one o'clock.

Ned spent the morning with Nina, and quite enjoyed her company. He was also impressed (and delighted) to find out that she lived in Brooklyn and was only in Russia visiting relatives because of a death in the family. They made plans to see each other back in the States.

When the men assembled at the helicopter, Ned asked Semyon what was going on. He told him that it was nothing. They had just caught a guy stealing from Viktor. According to Semyon, one of Viktor's varied business interests involved stealing luxury cars, stripping them down and sending the parts to China where they were painstakingly reassembled and resold at a ridiculous profit. One of Viktor's men had found out that this guy, Ivan, had been sending steering assemblies without the airbags. He had set up his own very lucrative business through which he sold the airbags online.

"It's bad," Semyon said. "I actually know the guy. He's lots of fun. But business is business and he has to be made an example of. I just hope it's not too bad."

In the helicopter, Ned couldn't help feel almost overwhelmed by the bonhomie and good cheer of his fellow passengers. Grigori and Evgeni were speaking English with him, joking about Nina and telling stories about Viktor's amazing wealth and power. Even Vasilly said, "Viktor is a very successful man" in English, though he didn't look at Ned.

They flew over a lot of farms and woods and the occasional town. They set down in what appeared to be a large and abandoned parking lot. About fifty yards away, there were two burly men in suits, one armed with an AK-47, and both leaning against a big, red Mitsubishi SUV. The unarmed one, who was smoking, walked over to the helicopter as the rotors slowed down. He was smiling and looked very casual.

When the helicopter doors opened, he greeted Grigori like an old friend and said hello to the others. As they spoke rather animatedly, Semyon gave Ned a condensed translation. "Grigori and Ilya are old friends. Grigori says he is too old for this shit, that's he's too senior. Ilya says Viktor said he had to be there, because of the American friend—hey, that's you. Grigori agrees and tells Ilya that they should just go ahead and get it over with."

Grigori, who must've heard every word Semyon said, turned around and yelled at his group in English. "Let's go, the sooner we get done, the sooner we can get out of this place."

Ilya led them over to the Mitsubishi. The guy with the AK-47 nodded and acknowledged Grigori. Then he opened one of the truck's rear doors. Inside, there was a small man tied up with duct tape over his mouth. His blue-and-yellow face indicated that he had been beaten up quite a while ago and the dried blood on the front of his shirt showed that it had been quite brutal. He seemed unconscious even though the one eye that wasn't too puffed up to see was wide open. Suddenly, Grigori barked out, "Macnair, Evgeni, take him out."

Ned, taking Evgeni's lead, grabbed the small man and helped pull him from the vehicle. They stood him up between them. His head didn't come to Ned's chin and he felt light as a child. Following Grigori, they frog-marched the unfortunate man through an iron gate in the high wall beside the parking lot.

Inside, Ned could see that it was a cemetery. But it was unlike any he had ever seen. Instead of simple crosses or inscribed tombstones, all of these graves had fountains and statutes. Some even had huge granite blocks with what appeared to be the life-sized photographs of young men in suits etched into them. They dragged the tied-up man (who was no longer even attempting to walk with them) around a corner to a sumptuous tomb. Not only was there a life-sized granite statue of a young man, but there was also one of a slick Mercedes-Benz convertible.

As they approached, Grigori himself grabbed the small man and threw him down in front of the tomb. Then he started yelling something in Russian. Semyon grabbed Ned and pulled him back a few feet, then started telling him what was going on. "He's calling him a stupid bastard . . . told him he had it made, and that he fucked it all up . . . And now he's telling him about Valeri, who's buried right here, telling him how this man, this honorable man, died for the cause, died an honest man and that he could have been just like him. He says that he wanted the last thing he ever saw in his miserable little life was the beautiful grave of a man who deserved respect . . . And now he's telling him that he'll be buried in a cardboard box if anyone even bothers to bury him at all."

The thief started shaking and crying. He tried to get up, but Grigori threw him roughly back down. Unbidden, Vasilly came out of the group. With his left hand, he grabbed the man by his collar and brought him up to a kneeling position. He then pulled out his knife and sliced the screaming man's eyeballs.

Ned couldn't help flinching. He heard one of the Russians—he couldn't be sure which—laugh as the man tried to stand up and stumbled screaming to the ground.

Semyon took Ned away, and they all started walking back to the Mitsubishi and the helicopter. Most of the Russians were chatting, but Ned couldn't speak. Finally, he quietly asked Semyon, "That was for me to see, right? To teach me not to steal?"

"It was for all of us," Semyon answered. "You think you're the only one who handles money?"

Ned sighed. "If this is what you guys do to a thief," he said, "I'd hate to see what you do to a rat."

Semyon looked at Ned with a face that showed both shock and suspicion. "We have no rats here. There is nobody to tell—those police we do not own are scared to death of us," he said. "This is not America."

Ned did his best to smile. "Oh, I know that, my friend," he said, and watched as friendliness rewashed over Semyon's face. "And you're right, we Americans are lazy. We just would have killed the guy."

Semyon shrugged and nodded. "Sure, but then nobody learns anything," he said. "A body is just a body. This guy, though, he can go tell his friends what happens to people who steal from Viktor."

Ned looked ahead at the guys he was with. Even though the blinded man's screams could still be heard behind them, no one was in a hurry to leave the scene. Instead, they looked loose, jocular, even proud. If anything, they looked like a sports team, joking and laughing after an easy victory.

At that moment, Ned realized he was halfway around the world, surrounded by a vicious gang. He took a deep breath to calm his mind. His charade had to be as convincing as the illusions in the oil paintings—without the heroics.

Chapter Twelve

Ned was surprised at how much he liked Moscow. So far, he had come to see it as a huge, ugly and even soulless city. But now that he was exploring the historic parts of the city with Nina, he had come to see Moscow as an entirely different place, full of life and culture. She was staying in a hotel near Red Square, and Ned joined her for a couple of days before her flight back to New York.

She showed him a city of wonder and beauty. She took him to sites of mainly pre-Communist interest—museums, cathedrals and the Iberian Gate. He was stunned to see such magnificence in a culture he had already written off as without taste or depth. As he was getting tired of Russian food, she took him to French, Italian and even Japanese restaurants.

He was sad to see her go, but Ned passed the rest of the week amiably enough with Semyon in his old neighborhood. He paid for his parents to go on vacation at a Black Sea resort and he and Ned had taken over their apartment. It wasn't as fun or as educational as staying with Nina, but he had a good time nevertheless. Semyon and his friends never seemed to do any work, but they had what seemed like a limitless amount of cash. They also seemed to be liked, or at least respected, by everyone they ran into. Ned realized that the respect they received may have been induced by fear, but it didn't really seem to matter.

The neighborhood itself was ugly—cramped, dirty, uniformly gray and without much variation in the shape, size or overall look of the buildings. But the people were unfailingly cheerful and Ned had a great time with them. He found the Uzbeks generally a warmer and friendlier people than the Russians, and he liked their food, especially the flavored rice dishes served with meat.

Although he was excited about the potential of seeing Nina again, Ned was more than a little sad about leaving. He had become something of a celebrity in Semyon's old neighborhood, and didn't want to go back to the anonymity and unfriendliness of his apartment building at home. Maybe, he thought to himself, with all his money coming in, he could move to a friendlier neighborhood or town even. Maybe something near a beach, or nearer to Brooklyn in case things worked out with Nina.

* * *

After the flight to Canada and the drive across the border, the men convened in Grigori's office. Grigori said something in Russian, and everybody except he, Vasilly and Ned left. After seeing the others leave, Ned started to get up, but stopped when Grigori told him to stay.

Grigori walked up to Ned much as he did when they first met, but this time he had a big smile on his face. Then Vasilly pulled up a chair and sat next to him, facing him.

That made Ned uneasy. Not only was Vasilly very close and facing him in what some might find an intrusive or even threatening manner, but Ned had developed a very visceral fear of Vasilly. It wasn't just that he had seen Vasilly do terrible things, it was that he had never seen him do anything else. Ned had gotten to the point at which he involuntarily associated the look of Vasilly's taut but impassive face as a threat to his very existence. Ned tried hard not to let his fear show and merely nodded in Vasilly's direction while pretending to listen hard to whatever Grigori was saying to him.

Grigori looked at him, smiled broadly and said something in Russian to Vasilly that Ned took to be an admonishment. Vasilly just smiled. "Macnair, I think you have a problem with Vasilly."

Ned looked over at him. Vasilly nodded without a trace of emotion.

"It seems," Grigori said in a grave-sounding voice, "that he lost a large sum of cash because of you."

Vasilly nodded.

"Yeah, he bet me that you wouldn't last five minutes in Russia," Grigori said. "But everybody there likes you, you did a wonderful job—and now he owes me money, so he blames you." He laughed uproariously at his own joke. Even Vasilly let out a small snort of a chuckle. Once the shock wore off, Ned couldn't help but laugh too.

"You make me very, very happy," Grigori said, putting his meaty hands on Ned's shoulders and kissing him on both cheeks. "Not only does import/export plan work, but I look like a genius for thinking of it." He went back behind his desk and opened the top left drawer. He then pulled out a handful of hundred-dollar bills and started throwing them one by one at Ned, laughing the whole time. Ned instinctively picked them up and collected them in his lap. Ned lost count long before he finished.

"Thank you," he said.

"No need to thank me," Grigori said. "You earned it. You do good work. You are okay."

"Thanks—I mean, it's great to be working with you," then Ned paused. "Is there anything else I need to do, like get a tattoo or something?"

Grigori laughed and Vasilly snorted in disgust. "No, no, no, don't worry," Grigori said. "You work for us, but you're not one of us—just like your little Uzbek friend."

Ned was puzzled.

"But don't worry," Grigori said. "It's still very good. You will get rich, you will have women, you will have our protection."

"Sounds sweet," said Ned.

"Go. The Uzbek will take you back to Delaware."

"But doesn't he want to go home to his wife and family?"

"No, I have met his wife," Grigori said. "He would be better off driving you home."

Ned laughed and got up to leave. "Wait," Grigori said. "You still owe Vasilly."

"How much?"

Vasilly looked him in the eye and said. "You decide."

Ned paused. "Well, I don't know how much your bet was for," he said. He counted off fifteen bills and offered them to Vasilly. Vasilly accepted the offering and smiled. "Didn't I tell you this boy was smart, Vasilly?" said Grigori loudly. "He knows it is much better to have friends than money, but he is smart enough to know that life with some money is much better than life with none." Vasilly grunted his assent. "Go now, Mr. Macnair," Grigori added. "Go make me lots of money."

* * *

Ned did as he was told. Back at Hawkridge, he resumed his post as the shipping/receiving manager. He did little work aside from ordering, receiving and rerouting coils from Eastern Europe. It was tedious work even when he did have something to do, and far more so when he had almost nothing to do. Katie and Juan—the people he was supposed to supervise—were very able and experienced at their jobs, and didn't need much from him. So Ned found himself filling his long days at the office talking to Nina or Semyon on the phone or looking up biker-related news on the Internet.

He would occasionally go out for lunch with Steve, the factory's floor manager, and from time to time, the Swede would join them. They had nothing but good things to say about Ned's work and were pleasantly surprised when he told them he'd like more responsibilities because he didn't have enough to do.

One day the package he received from Detroit hit his desk with a *clunk*. "Hmm, is he putting change in there now?" Ned asked absent-mindedly.

"How should I know?" answered the delivery kid in a surly way, then left.

Ned opened the envelope, poured out his cash and a pair of car keys. He looked at them. The stylized, embossed "L" on them indicated that they belonged to a Lexus. The simple key ring attached them to a small card. Written on it in black ink was an address: 84 Chaddwyck Blvd, New Castle. For the rest of the day, he wondered about the keys, worried about them, twirled them on his finger. He decided that after work was as good a time as any to deliver the keys.

* * *

It was an upscale neighborhood, full of large detached houses. The houses were new; in fact, Ned could tell the entire neighborhood was new because of the sparse-but-not-serene look that a lack of businesses and old-growth trees gave such places. Almost every house had an SUV or a minivan parked out front. A few had basketball nets or hockey goals in the driveways. Foot traffic was nonexistent, and the only movement he could see at all came from commuters coming home in more SUVs and minivans. He felt very conspicuous on the old Indian. When he got to 84 Chaddwyck, he was shocked to see it was a vacant lot. He checked again. The card said 84, but in between 82 and 86, was nothing but grass and weeds, a vacant lot. At the curb was a black Lexus SUV with a white parking ticket under one of the windshield wipers.

Ned pulled up behind the Lexus on the Indian. He got off the bike and walked up to the car. He instinctively looked around before sticking the key in the door. It opened. Ned got in, put the key in the ignition, and started it up. As it hummed to life, he heard the stereo spring to life. It was playing that horrible Eurodisco that Semyon favored. Ned put it all together. He called Semyon, after turning the stereo off. "Hey, man, what's up with this Lexus?" he asked. "Whose is it?"

"Yours man, all yours," Semyon laughed. "Grigori couldn't stand to see you riding around on that old piece of shit of yours, so he got you something."

"And it's legal?"

"Totally."

"In my name?"

"Yes, Mr. . . . uh . . . what is it again? Steakman?"

"Steadman, Eric Steadman," Ned was a touch concerned that Semyon had not done the transfer correctly. "You got it right, didn't you?"

"Yeah, yeah, Steadman," he said. "Ludmilla has all your information on file; she takes care of things like that for me . . . she's a saint, she is . . . but you gotta get your own insurance and plates, it's got dealer plates on now so you can drive it, but not for too long."

"Well, thanks—and thank Grigori and Ludmilla too." Ned paused. "I just thought of something. I rode out here on the Indian. How am I gonna get it home?"

"That's not important. Grigori wants you to get rid of it anyway," Semyon said, with a long pause. "He says it makes you too obvious. He wants you to look like a young businessman, not a biker."

Ned let out an exasperated sigh. "Is that so?"

"Yeah, that is so," Semyon answered sharply. "Didn't you tell me you knew a guy who wanted to buy it?"

"Yeah, a guy who works in the warehouse at Hawkridge."

"Then all is taken care of. You will wait there for ten minutes."

Ned hung up and reveled in the smell of new leather. He didn't have to wait quite ten minutes. A new Ford pickup pulled in behind the Indian. Ned got out of the Lexus. Then he heard the unmistakable rumble of a Sportster. It pulled up in front of the Lexus. Ned recognized the Lawbreaker right away.

The Lawbreaker nodded to the young man who was driving the pickup. "Give him the key," the biker said to Ned. "He'll take care of your piece of crap."

"Where are you taking it?"

"It'll be dropped in the parking lot of a place called Hawkridge. Now, don't waste any more of my time."

The biker and the driver of the pickup loaded the Indian on the bed. The Lawbreaker looked at Ned. "Open the glove box in the Lexus," he ordered.

Ned did as he was told and saw an envelope. He got out of the car and was about to open it when the biker seized his arm and took it. He looked hard at Ned for a few seconds.

"Okay, Johnny, it's yours."

Without another word, Johnny and the Lawbreaker headed off in different directions. Ned felt a chill in the evening air.

* * *

Heading into work a few days later, Ned saw the Swede and Dave waiting for him in the lobby. The Swede looked at Ned and told him that he could take the day off because Dave wanted to talk with him and that Katie would fill in for him. Dave was clearly angry, but the Swede gave Ned a warm-hearted-though-concerned look.

Dave refused to speak in the car. When they finally returned to his office, Ned was surprised to see two uniformed state troopers there. The two men followed them in. Dave sat behind his desk facing Ned. Ned noticed that one of the officers was operating a small video camera on a tripod.

After a short oath to tell the truth and to acknowledge that he knew the conversation was being recorded, Dave began. "I see you registered a new car."

"New to me, at least," Ned responded. "It's a 2008."

Dave shot him a hard look. "Yes, yes it is," he said. "A 2008 Lexus RX350. Now that would run in the thirty-to-thirty-five-thousand dollar area, I would expect."

"Yes, I believe it would."

"And you presumably paid for this vehicle."

"Yes."

"Do you have a receipt for this transaction?"

"Somewhere. I dunno. I was never too good with paperwork."

Dave sighed and rubbed his eyes with his palm. "Where did you get that kind of money? I have no record of a loan or line of credit in your name."

"It was a private loan."

"From who? You have no family, no friends. Who would loan you money?"

Ned thought fast. "The Swede. Against my salary."

"I can check that. And where did you buy it?"

"He arranged it."

"Really, he just happened to buy you a very expensive car from a dealer who I happen to know has a severe drug and even more severe debt problem."

"I don't know."

"And did you know that this dealer just happens to have connections with people we believe to be involved with organized crime?"

"No."

"Turn the camera off," Dave said to the cop, who did. "Look, Ned, this is your life that's at stake here. If you are out there playing gangster, tell me now and I can take care of you. These guys aren't like bikers."

"I don't know who you're talking about. All I did was buy a car."

"Fine, turn the camera back on." Then he turned back to Ned, and said, "Ned Aiken—also known as Eric Steadman—it is my duty to inform you that while you are not currently under arrest, the FBI will conduct an investigation into this matter, which could lead to criminal charges and/or expulsion from the witness protection program."

Ned let that last remark sink in, and rubbed his face with his hands. "Am I free to go?"

Dave turned the camera off himself. "For now," he answered.

* * *

Ned was so concerned with the day's events that he did not see Semyon's car outside. As soon as he parked the big Lexus, he heard his friend shouting at him jubilantly. "Hey, hey!" he shouted. "Do you love it? It's beautiful. Could use a little color, though."

"Yeah," Ned said brusquely. "But it's more trouble than it's worth."

"Waddaya mean?"

"A—uh—a cop came and asked me about it," Ned answered. "Said something about how the dealer was involved with drugs and 'organized crime.'"

"Don't worry about cops," Semyon assured him. "Aren't you gonna invite me in?"

Once inside, Semyon did his best to calm Ned down. He told him that he knew what was going on. The car dealer was a guy named Adrian Blake who had a bit of a coke problem. He fell deep into debt with a

friend of Grigori's and was allowed to pay off much of
the balance by selling cars at sweetheart prices to those
he owed. "I think we ended up paying five hundred dollars for yours," Semyon said. "He puts it in the books as
a thirty-two-thousand-dollar sale and when the bank
comes asking for their money he says he doesn't have
it. He goes bankrupt and starts all over again with the
cash in his pocket. It works out for everyone."

"The dealer," he continued, "this Blake character, is
man who takes way too much powder up his nose and
now he doesn't want to pay for it. In any other country
he would be dead, but here he just loses his business
and goes through American bankruptcy. For one year
he lives like a poor man, then he goes back to where he
started from—or maybe he'll go to an American jail for
six months for fraud. Either way he is lucky, very lucky."

Ned, sick of hearing how "the rest of the world"
does things, just glared at him. The look on Semyon's
face made it clear that he had no idea what Ned's problem was. They talked about Ned's new car and about
the old Kia and how he'd be much better served to live
in a better place in a better neighborhood. He was considered one of "the friends" now and deserved to show
off a little.

Ned lightened up and smiled. While it was true that
his organized crime connections had gained him the

luxury car, it was unlikely Dave could connect the two enough to stand up in court. And if he was any good as a cop, he wouldn't be babysitting guys in the witness protection program. He asked Semyon what was up.

"If you worked the weekend at Hawkridge, how much would you make?"

"I don't know, a few hundred bucks, why?"

"How would you like to make twenty-five hundred and maybe more."

"Sounds good," Ned said. "What would we have to do?"

Semyon smiled. He knew his partner was in. "Super easy. All we have to do is deliver a package from the port at Elizabeth, New Jersey, to Roman in Long Island," he said with a shrug. "It's a special package. Grigori says he gets them from time to time and that it requires special care."

"What's so special that it needs two men to escort it?" Ned asked. "I mean, this is a guy who sends heroin through FedEx. What could be so valuable that he needs us to transport it?"

"My guess is that it's art. These guys—these rich guys—all have lots and lots of art," Semyon said. "They really like to collect beautiful things."

Chapter Thirteen

The port at Elizabeth, New Jersey, looked depressing and uninviting. It was flat and full of low, wide, gray buildings. Power lines were everywhere. Signs of life, apart from parked cars and the ubiquitous gulls, were absent. Off in the distance, Ned could see an iron bridge that looked like the skeleton of some giant snake. The asphalt was searing under the oppressive sun and the lack of trees and grass made the oppressive heat seem far worse. The walk from the car to the office was truly miserable.

Semyon was droning on, complaining about something, but Ned wasn't listening. He was thinking instead about how he had already called Dave twice to get permission to take another trip and had gotten no answer. Ned knew that if he was caught out of state without authorization again, the shit would truly hit the fan.

Once inside the office, Ned and Semyon were greeted by a small, dark man with deeply set eyes who appeared to know Semyon, but not well. He led them to and up a ship's gangway. It was a sturdy and large ocean-going freighter. Ned did not recognize the flag the ship flew, but the crew all appeared to be Indian or Bangladeshi. The small man led them across the deck into a hatch on the ship's bridge.

They traveled down a circular staircase into a corridor with a number of hatches on each side. A couple were open, and Ned could see a number of bunk beds inside one and a small kitchen in the other. At the end of the corridor was a small room with a cot. On the walls were crude drawings of sea creatures, including an octopus and what appeared to be a dolphin. As they entered, a young girl, perhaps ten years old, emerged from behind the door.

"That's the package," said the small man. "Don't worry, she is absolutely untouched," he added and smiled lasciviously. "Roman will be very, very pleased."

Ned was dumbstruck. Semyon recovered more quickly. "Thanks," he said. "Is it already paid for?" The small man nodded, and Semyon handed him a small wad of bills for his trouble. He then leaned down and spoke to the girl in Russian. She shook her head and started speaking in a language that sounded kind of like Russian to Ned, but that he could tell was somewhat different. She said a couple of words that sounded like *ar mesmis* over and over again. Semyon sighed in frustration, shrugged and rolled his eyes at Ned and gestured to the girl to follow him off the ship. She indicated she understood and grabbed a small bag from under the cot before following him out. Semyon instructed Ned to be last in line.

When they reached the car, Semyon opened the right front door and stepped in. Ned opened the right rear door and gestured for the little girl to hop in. She seemed utterly confused and Ned had to secure her seatbelt. She flinched when he brushed against her.

Ned closed her door and started to drive without saying anything. He glared at Semyon who attempted to smile, shrugged again and looked out his window. The girl, wide-eyed and silent, looked around the car and out the window. She seemed terrified, but also excited.

They were almost on I-95 before anyone spoke.
Finally, Ned shouted, "What . . . the . . . fuck?"

Semyon shrugged again. "I guess this is the package we have to deliver to Roman," he said. "To tell you
the truth, I'm not actually all that surprised. I've heard
things."

"I repeat . . . what the fuck?"

"She is a prize—for Roman," Semyon replied. "You
know—to do *women's work*."

"I'm pretty sure 'women's work' doesn't mean cooking and cleaning." Ned was shouting so much he felt
like he had to pull over to the shoulder, but he realized
that Semyon had vodka on him for sure and certainly a
few weapons and that they also had an undocumented
minor in the car. Even if he told on every Russian he
knew and then some, he would be looking at prison
time. Instead, he took the next exit, Wilson Avenue,
into Newark. He'd always heard Newark was a shithole,
but it didn't look that bad—certainly no worse than
Elizabeth. They stopped at the deserted corner of Wilson
and Rome. Ned looked Semyon in the eye and angrily
demanded, "What is she, fucking nine years old?"

"I don't know."

"Ask her!"

"I can't."

"Why not?"

"She's from Georgia."

"What?"

"Not Atlanta, *Jawja, y'all*." Semyon was getting angry himself. "It's not far from Chechnya. They call themselves *Kartveli*, but English and Americans call it 'Georgia' after some king or something. Assholes."

The little girl seemed to notice the word "Kartveli" and perked up.

"So? You've talked to all kinds of . . ." Ned was at a loss for words, ". . . Khazaks, Tajiks, Estonians and all kinds of others . . ."

"Yeah, but they all spoke Russian."

"And she doesn't?"

"She was probably born at least a dozen years after the Georgians kicked the Russians out."

"So, the languages can't be that different."

"Stop being an American! The Georgian language is like none other in the world!" Semyon was shouting. "Their word for mother is *dede* and their word for father is *mama*! It's totally crazy."

On hearing two more familiar words, the little girl started chattering nervously. Ned looked back and he could see that her eyes were still wide enough so that he could see the tops and bottoms of her irises and that she wasn't quite focusing on anything in particular. She tightly held onto her small bag of belongings. Semyon shushed her. He smiled at her and made some funny faces and hand gestures. She didn't exactly laugh, but she did do her best to put on a little smile. He put both hands on his chest and said "Semyon" a couple of times. She got the message and similarly introduced herself as "Sopho." Semyon grinned broadly and smacked Ned. "Macnair!" he shouted in obvious mock anger. Sopho did her best to laugh. She tried to pronounce Macnair and came nowhere close. Semyon laughed. She seemed to appreciate that.

Ned marveled at the power Semyon had. Here was a little girl, kidnapped (or sold by her family), thousands of miles away from home and about to be sold into slavery, almost feeling comfortable. Ned had always known that Semyon had a degree of charm, but when he realized that part of the reason he had such a good rapport with Sopho was that he had children of his own. That actually enraged him. "Semyon, you bastard," he said. "How can you do that? You know where she's going. What if she was one of your kids?" Sopho looked at Ned with fear. He realized that he had made himself look like the bad guy with his outbursts, and had, by extension, made Semyon look like the good guy, her potential savior.

"She *isn't* one of my kids, thank God," Semyon said. "Listen, you can't think that way, you can't get soft. This is Roman's property, we can't ask, we can't judge."

"Ours is not to reason why . . ."

"What?

"Nothing," Ned's head was in his hands. Sopho was still chattering, eyes wide open, almost certainly aware that neither of them had any idea what she was saying. Ned sighed.

"So, do you know any more Georgian?"

"Kartveli," Semyon corrected. "Just a few swear-words . . . oh, and hello is *gamarjoba* and good-bye is *nakhvamdis.*"

"Gamarjoba!" said the girl brightly.

Ned grinned. "Gamarjoba," he said sadly, then turned to Semyon. "Let's get the fuck out of here."

Just as he was about to turn the key, he heard his phone ring. Semyon shot him a serious look. Despite his better judgment, Ned hoped it was Dave. It wasn't. It was Katie from the office. Her upbeat tone angered Ned. "Hey, Eric," she said in a sing-song voice. "How are you?"

"I've been better."

"Oh, I'm sorry to hear that," she giggled, even though nobody had said anything remotely funny. "Just a couple of things here at the office . . ."

Ned regrouped. "Really? What's up?" he asked in as close to normal a voice as he could muster.

"Nothing really," she said. "We got twice as many coils from Romania as Steve ordered . . ."

"Yeah."

"So I sent some of the extra ones up to Mr. Andersson."

"What?"

"Mr. Andersson, he's at a trade show at the Jacob Javits Center up there in Manhattan," she said. "I thought he could use them to show his customers."

Ned felt cold run through his veins. He collected himself and asked, "Which half?"

"The second half, I think. I'm not really sure," Katie replied, paused and added an insincere giggle. "And there were some men here looking for you."

"What?"

"Yeah, a couple of guys," she said. "They didn't say much—just that they wanted to see you . . . in person."

Ned breathed deeply. "Fine," he said. "What did they look like?"

"Big guys," she said. "Lots of tattoos. One of them had a tattoo of a spade—you know, from like a deck of cards—on his wrist. Anyone you know?"

Ned sighed. He didn't know anyone with such a tat, but he also knew that the Ace of Spades was a very important part of Sons of Satan imagery. He knew that, in all likelihood, any pair of men visiting him at work were either cops or bikers, and cops generally didn't tattoo their wrists. "I'm not sure," he told her. "Did they say anything?"

"Not much, really, just said they wanted to see you and when I asked them what they wanted they said it wasn't related to Hawkridge," she said brightly. "Are they friends of yours?"

"Probably."

"Anyways, I thought you should know."

Ned thanked her and said good-bye. He could feel his blood pressure rise. He turned to Semyon. "I gotta see the Swede."

"No way, we're headed east to New York," he snapped. "Not back in time to Delaware."

"No, no, it's cool, he's in Manhattan—at the Javits for a trade show," Ned answered. "We can see him *after* we take care of Roman."

"Now you're talking sense."

Ned started driving. Sopho finally stopped talking and started to look out the window. Semyon thanked Ned again for coming to his senses. They were approaching I-95 when Ned noticed two Harley-Davidsons behind him. They were bikers. Ned could tell immediately. Their faces were too small in the rear-view mirror for him to even try to recognize, and they weren't wearing any colors, just orange-and black Harley jackets—but he could tell they were bikers.

He changed lanes. They changed with him. He sped up to about ninety. They followed suit. Semyon, drinking out of his familiar Evian bottle, didn't notice anything. Sopho was still looking out the windows at the huge trucks and the passing countryside. Ned brought the car onto an off-ramp that led into the Ironbound neighborhood on the other side of Newark. Semyon looked at him with a raised eyebrow. "Gas," Ned assured him. "And food for the package. God knows when she last ate."

Semyon giggled awkwardly. It was clear he was happy that Ned was going along with the task ahead of them, but he, too, had his misgivings.

Ned looked in the mirror. The bikers had also taken the off-ramp, and had actually closed ground on them. Ned looked back at Semyon. "You go in the store and get some food and drinks—stuff kids like," he said. "And I'll get the gas."

Semyon nodded, and said something to Sopho in Russian. She just looked at him in a fearful silence, then started talking nervously in her own language. He chuckled and told Ned that he was just checking to see if she was faking about knowing any Russian. "What I told her was fucking hilarious," he said. "If she understood even just a few words of Russian, she'd be laughing so hard she'd fall out of her seat."

They pulled into a Hess station and Ned went to the pump farthest from the convenience store. Without another word, Semyon got out of the car and started trudging toward the store. Ned opened his door and Sopho started talking excitedly, as though she was scared to be alone again. Ned put one leg on the ground, and looked behind him. He saw the two bikers getting off their Harleys. A second later, they were approaching him.

Ned pulled his leg back into the car and slammed his door shut. He restarted the Lexus and laid rubber out of the gas station. Sopho started screaming. She undid her seatbelt and jumped between the two front seats. She was hitting Ned, not trying to hurt him, just to get his attention, as though he had forgotten about Semyon. She was crying and pointing back at the convenience store until she ran out of breath. Then she slumped back into her seat, silently. Ned scanned the rearview mirror and was relieved that the bikers were not coming after him.

He hurried to get back on I-95. Just before the on-ramp, he stopped and got out of the car. Sopho started screaming. He opened up her door, and she stopped screaming and started chattering in a nervous way that made Ned think she was asking questions. He fastened her seatbelt, closed the door and got back in the driver's seat. He looked at Sopho and smiled. She didn't smile back, but seemed to calm down a little.

Ned took 95 south, toward Delaware. About forty-five minutes of silent driving in which Ned ran ideas through his head stressfully and Sopho looked out the window sadly, Ned turned off into a pleasant enough little blue-collar town called Burlington. He parked behind a chrome-trimmed diner on High Street and gestured for Sopho to follow him inside.

They took a booth with a window through which Ned could see their car and sat down. He ordered bacon and eggs with coffee for himself and a cheeseburger with fries and a Coke for her. The older, heavy-set waitress spoke to Sopho, who did not answer back. The waitress then shot a questioning look at Ned. "She's deaf," he said. The waitress apologized.

When the food arrived, Ned was too stressed to eat his. Sopho ate hers quickly but politely. She started to talk in her own language again, perhaps to thank Ned for the meal. Ned noticed the waitress and a man she had been talking with stop and stare suspiciously at them. Ned put his fingers to his lips in an effort to silence Sopho. She got the picture. He then got up and escorted her to the washroom, realizing she probably wouldn't know how to get there herself and wouldn't have the ability to ask. He waited nervously outside, hoping she wouldn't climb out the window to escape and watched the waitress and her friend talk about the pair of them. After a few minutes, Sopho re-emerged and Ned took her back to the booth. The waitress walked quickly and forcefully to their table, and put down the bill with a thud. Ned looked up, she was glaring at him. "Well, I hope you and *your daughter* enjoyed your meal," she said sternly.

"Thank you," Ned said angrily. "We did."

"I know it's not my place to say anything," she continued. "But she don't sound like no deaf person I ever heard—sounds foreign—and she don't do the sign language either."

Ned stared at her. He was trying to formulate a story when he realized that he had bigger fish to fry than to rationalize his situation to some fat, suburban New Jersey egg-slinger. He sighed, looked her in the eye and said, "You're absolutely right. It's not your place." Then he pulled out a twenty, put it on the table, got up and gestured for Sopho to come with him.

After a moment of stunned silence, the waitress yelled after him. "I know you're up to something, mister. Something no good," she shouted. "And Dan here, his brother's a trooper, so you just watch out."

Ned and Sopho got back into the car. He looked at her and wondered what people would think when they saw the two of them together. She didn't look too out of place in New Jersey if she kept her mouth shut. Her clothes were not as flashy or covered in logos as most of the kids in the area (and a little threadbare), but she could probably pass as an ordinary, if perhaps poor, kid. She was actually too old to be his daughter in any realistic scenario—and she didn't look anything like him anyway. And when she opened her mouth it was clear she was from some place far away.

His phone rang. It was Semyon or someone using Semyon's phone. Just as likely, one of the bikers had taken it and was calling him with it. Either way, answering it was not a great idea. When it stopped ringing, Ned called Dave. No answer. So he called Nina. She answered on the second ring. "Nina," Ned said. "It's me. I really, really need your help."

There was a pause. Ned figured that since their phone conversations had been light and their entire relationship was based on their shared, tacit decision not to talk about the darker sides of their professions or their friends that she wasn't excited about the idea of having a serious talk. "Really?" she finally asked, sounding suspicious. "What's the problem?"

"I have a delivery to make—for Roman."

"So, deliver it," she sounded angry. "No more problem."

"No, Nina, you don't understand," Ned pleaded. "The package is a little girl."

He heard Nina groan. "So deliver the package."

"What? Are you nuts?" Ned yelled. "She's just a kid! Not even ready for junior high!"

"Calm down," she sounded stern. "If you are trying to prove to me that you are a good guy, stop. This is not a Hollywood movie and you are not a hero. You have a job to do."

"But she's just a kid . . ."

"I'm sure she is, but you have a job to do and if you don't, you will die," her voice softened, but still sounded cynical. "Besides, if he loses this one, he'll just go get another. Do your job, Macnair, save yourself."

He hung up.

He looked back at Sopho. He smiled and made a funny face at her. She gave a sort of half smile to acknowledge his effort.

Something caught Ned's eye. The waitress and her friend had come outside and were now writing down his license plate number. Ned realized that they were going to call the trooper. At least, he thought to himself, he had less than an hour left in New Jersey until he got into Pennsylvania.

He started the car again and rejoined I-95 south. After a few miles, he took the Chichester exit to Marcus Hook. He drove down the divided lanes of Market Street to Dave's office. For the first time in his memory, he really wanted to be there. Dave may have given him a hard time, but the FBI had saved his life once before, and he was in a much tougher predicament this time.

Parked outside, he took Sopho out of the car and walked up to the outside door. It was always unlocked during business hours. They walked upstairs, Ned in front, and came to Dave's office door. Ned was surprised to see it ajar. "Hello," he called out. "Dave, are you here?"

No answer. Ned turned and looked at Sopho. She looked very afraid. He gestured for her to stay exactly where she was. A wave of desperate fear washed over her face, and she pleaded "*Ara, ara.*" Ned had no idea what she meant, but knew she didn't want to stay put. He put on his sternest face and made it clear she had to. She finally nodded.

He turned and went into Dave's office. Dave was at his desk with his back to Ned. "Hey, Dave," Ned said cautiously. "Everything okay?"

No answer. Ned tenuously approached Dave. As he got closer, he could see that his file was open on Dave's computer. Ned smelled blood. He looked down and could see that the carpet was stained reddish brown. He got closer to Dave, turned him around and saw that his throat had been slit ear to ear, his white-collared blue shirt drenched with blood. Ned looked at Dave's PC— his complete file was up on the monitor. It included his address, the make, model and license plate of his car, his employer, everything. He was an open book. He was as good as dead whether he delivered the girl or not.

He rushed out of the office and put his arm around Sopho, nearly carrying her as he ran down the stairs. Ned almost threw her into the back seat of the Lexus. He jumped into the driver's seat and headed toward the Interstate. He had to get rid of the Lexus. But he also knew he had to get to Manhattan. If, he decided, he could get to the heroin-filled coils, he could prove that the Russians were smuggling drugs into the country. Otherwise, he'd have to explain why his FBI caseworker was dead and what he was doing with an undocumented little girl. Without the drugs, it was just his word against the Russians', and his past as a snitch would do him more harm than good. Instead of heading to the Interstate, he took Highway 13 south to Wilmington. The bikers or Russians would be looking for him on the Interstate, and if that stupid waitress had actually called the troopers, they'd be there too.

He stopped at a Suzuki dealer in Edgemoor, just across the state line, and bought two full-face motor-cycle helmets—one for himself and the other for Sopho. He also got her a jacket. Then he took the Lexus up to Hawkridge and parked in back of the warehouse. He got out of the Lexus as quietly as he could, and gestured for Sopho to do the same.

The old Indian he'd sold to Katie's boyfriend, Matt, was parked at the back of the lot. As Ned had both feared and predicted, Matt had already customized it. What had been a painstaking attempt to match the original red and brown two-tone color scheme had been painted over. The gas tank now a featured a portrait of a Viking warrior so drenched in lacquer that the paint job looked to be about an inch thick.

Ned handed Sopho her helmet and instructed her to get on the back seat of the Indian. She shook her head. She was clearly scared to ride on the big bike. Ned gave her a stern look. She made a timid step toward the bike, but stopped and started crying. Frustrated, Ned sighed and picked the girl up. He was surprised at how little she weighed and how violently she was shivering. He told her as soothingly as possible that everything was going to be all right. He put her helmet on her, adjusted the strap, then climbed on the bike and put his own on. He noticed that she instinctively put her tiny arms around him and held on. She still held onto her little bag as well.

Ned still had a spare key to the Indian on his key ring. He hadn't kept it from Matt intentionally; he had just never gotten around to giving it to him. He turned it. He knew that the sound of the kick start would immediately get the attention of anyone within earshot—Matt could even catch him and beat the shit out of him or hold him until the police came—so Ned was determined to get it on the first try. With his left foot on the peg, he stood up and put all his weight on the starter. The old motor gave out a disappointing *blub-blub-blub*.

"C'mon, baby," Ned whispered. He pushed Sopho back and tried again. This time it just began to take and then noisily crapped out. One of the Mexican guys Ned remembered from the warehouse stepped out of the loading dock doors to take a look. As soon as he saw Ned and Sopho on the big old bike he ran inside. Ned knew he was fetching Matt. With one last desperate kick, the dynamo ignited and the Indian roared to life. Ned pulled back on the accelerator and popped the clutch. Sopho flew backwards, nearly off the bike, but was saved by the ridiculous sissy bar Matt had since installed. She bounced back into Ned and held on as tightly as she could. Ned could neither see nor hear Matt and his friends running out of the loading dock and shouting at him to come back.

Ned went as fast as he could to Highway 13. He laughed a bit to himself when he thought of the picture they made: a man and a child in full-face neon-colored racer helmets riding on an incredibly loud vintage bike with a shiny Viking on each side of the gas tank—hardly the least conspicuous way to get to New York City. But he also knew he had no choice.

He eventually merged onto I-95 in Philadelphia. When traffic became too clogged, he split the lanes, driving between the anxious, waiting cars. It was illegal but it also allowed him to get into New Jersey in about half the time it would have taken if he had followed traffic laws. Sure that the Russians would expect him to visit Nina, he avoided Staten Island and the other quick routes into Brooklyn. Instead, he headed up the Palisades Parkway to the George Washington Bridge. Racing back down the West Side Highway, he took the 50th Street exit and parked the bike as legally as he could on 48th Street in front of a rental-car franchise.

He walked the rest of the way to the Javits Center down 11th Avenue past the dozens of luxury car dealerships that line the way. He was pulling Sopho by the hand and could tell that she was overwhelmed.

When they entered the huge glass rectangle that is the Javits, it was full of thousands of men and women—most of them in suits, but some in more casual clothes—milling around signs advertising the presence of the Annual Heating, Ventilation and Air Conditioning Professionals' Conference. Ned bypassed the line and went right to the exhibition floor's entrance. He was stopped by a security guard. The guard was tall and fat, with a small mouth that hung open all the time. Although he was only twenty-five or so, he was already mostly bald and already attempting to remedy the situation with a poor comb-over. "Can't let you in without a badge, sir," he said officiously.

"But this is an emergency," Ned told him, hoping his look of desperation would help convince the guy give him a break. "I need to get in there, to talk with an exhibitor."

"The only way in is with a badge," the young man actually appeared to be enjoying Ned's desperation.

"Fine," Ned said, exasperated. Other people in line behind him were getting angry at the hold up, and letting him know. "How do I get a badge?"

"Well, you should have signed up a month ago, then it only would have been $295," the guard said dully. "But now, you're gonna have to go over to the line 'way over there, register, show some ID and pay."

His superior, a plump black woman in her forties cut him off. "What's the problem here, Laderoute?" she demanded, looking back and forth at the security guard and Ned.

"This guy's got no badge," Laderoute said sheepishly. "And he wants to get in."

Betting that the older security guard was not only smarter, but also kinder than her charge, Ned appealed directly to her. "I'm not here for the show," he told her in measured tones. "I just have to talk with Thor Andersson of Hawkridge. It's an emergency."

"Mr. Andersson? I know him," the woman smiled. "What's the emergency? Maybe I can pass him a message."

"Some of the items he has may be potentially dangerous if they are mounted the wrong way," Ned stammered, thinking while he was talking. "Only someone familiar with the technology can help him . . . It could be a matter of life and death."

The older security guard looked at Ned and then at Sopho. Then she turned to Laderoute. "Do you think this man would bring his child along to see a ventilation trade show and make up a story about dangerous parts just to get out of paying the entry fee?" She turned back to Ned and told him to "go ahead" and admonished him to be back within fifteen minutes or he'd have to pay full price for a badge.

Ned let out an enormous sigh of relief and walked in, towing Sopho behind him. Inside was a huge set of rows of displays from various heating, ventilation and air-conditioning suppliers and related companies. Some were just wooden desks, while others looked like the sets of some elaborate game show in which all the prizes were air conditioners. There were hundreds of them. Finding Hawkridge shouldn't be too hard, he thought to himself, because it was one of the biggest such companies around, but with so many others there and with the Swede's desire to avoid anything ostentatious, it could take a long time.

Ned decided to be methodical. He started at one corner and walked straight down the long aisle. Sopho was still holding his hand and chattering quietly to herself in her language. He looked at her and marveled at how calm she looked. He wondered if her crossing had been so frightening that she just didn't have the emotional reserves left over to be scared now or that she was still young enough to believe that all adults had her best interest at heart. He wished for a moment that she spoke English. Before continuing their search for Hawkridge's booth, he went back to the snack bar near the entrance.

He bought a hot dog and a couple of slices of pizza. There was no place to sit in the crowded eating area, so he leaned against the wall while Sopho sat at his feet. She ate both slices of pizza and really seemed to enjoy her large orange soda. Ned relaxed for just a second and smiled at her. As he looked up, something familiar caught his eye. He couldn't be one-hundred percent sure it was Vasilly, but the man who walked past had on the same type of suit, was about the same size and had the same haircut. And his purposeful stride caused Ned's own spine to shiver. He did his best to hide behind some guys in suits who were talking loudly about "green technology."

As soon as the man who may have been Vasilly was out of sight, Ned grabbed Sopho—her hands still slightly greasy from the pizza—and walked in the opposite direction. He walked as quickly as he could without being totally obvious, and checked each stand to see if it was Hawkridge's. At the very end of the hall, he turned to go down the next aisle and saw—no more than twenty feet in front of him—two very large men in full Sons of Satan colors. Without thinking, he jumped—tugging Sopho off her feet—into the next aisle.

Then he stopped. He simply couldn't think of what to do next. The Sons were there and they obviously weren't buying air conditioners. They were in the building with just one purpose, as was Vasilly. Between the two of them, one was sure to succeed. He began to think his plan to grab the heroin-filled coils was stupid, doomed from the start. He should have just delivered the girl and kept on going. He looked at Sopho. She smiled weakly back up at him. He was trying to think of what he could possibly do next when he felt a big hand on his right shoulder. He wanted to scream, but couldn't. Instead, he turned around.

It was the Swede. He had a grave look on his face. "You should get out of here," he said.

"You have the wrong coils."

"I know," the Swede told him calmly. "And they have been disposed of. But your presence here is compromising us." The crowd walked past them, carrying on their own conversations and ignoring the scene unfolding in front of them.

"Disposed of?" Ned stammered. "So they're gone."

"Yes, they are," the Swede said. "And I had a talk with Grigori. We have a situation to manage." Then he gritted his teeth and said, "He told me that Roman is very displeased with you."

"Yeah," Ned said and gestured to Sopho.

Andersson sighed. "I had heard such stories about Roman, but did not want to believe them. I can't tolerate this sort of thing," he said. "Give me the girl. The authorities will ask me fewer questions."

"But they saw me come in with her, thousands of people have seen you and me talking."

"Just go. Here." Andersson pulled out a handful of business cards and selected one. He handed it to Ned. "This guy owes me a favor. Get in touch with him," he said. "I can't guarantee anything, but it's the best I can do."

Ned thanked him and said good-bye to Sopho. Her eyes fixed on him; he knew he'd never forget that look.

He scanned the crowd quickly for the two bikers and, failing to see them, walked as inconspicuously as he could toward the main entrance. He had taken just four steps when he heard Vasilly. "Come with me, Macnair," he said. "We have some things to talk about."

Ned could feel himself trembling. He turned and looked Vasilly in the eyes. After a long pause, he answered. "Go with you so you can kill me?" he finally said. "I don't think so."

Vasilly laughed. "If I wanted to kill you, you'd be dead already," he said and did his best to contort his mouth into an imitation of a smile. "You think I'm afraid of a few stupid security guards?"

"So why do you want me?"

"Grigori wants to talk with you. This issue with Roman is not a big deal," he said. "Maybe everyone makes a new start."

Ned knew he had no real options. He nodded and said, "Okay, let's go."

Vasilly smiled and started to walk through the building just a step behind him. Ned looked back at the quiet, angry man. "How's Semyon?" he asked.

Vasilly looked at him and curled the right side of his mouth into a grin. "He'll be alright," he said. "The bikers let him go; it seems like there was a mistaken identity. They were looking for a man named Ned Aiken, not Jared Macnair, or even Eric Steadman."

Ned's body sank. He thought about the tortured thief in Moscow. Just as Ned was trying to come to terms with that, he was grabbed from behind and spun around. Ned didn't recognize his face, but saw he was wearing full Sons of Satan colors and could tell from the patches on his jacket that he had killed for the club at least once before. "Fuckhead," was all the biker said. Then, "You're coming with us."

Vasilly glared at the biker and his partner, who was in front of them, blocking their way out. "Get out of our way," he snarled. "We have important business to attend to."

"No fuckin' way," said the second biker.

"Listen, you are too young to die over such trivial matters," Vasilly said. "Get out of our way, or you will pay severely."

The security guard from the entrance, Laderoute, approached the arguing men. "What's the trouble here?" he asked with as much command as he could muster. Then he looked at Ned. "And you," he said. "Your fifteen minutes are up. Time to go, buddy."

All five men stared at one another in stunned silence. Finally, Ned reared back and punched Vasilly as hard as he could in the jaw. The smaller man fell into the two bikers, but was agile enough to pull out a tiny Smith & Wesson handgun and shoot the security guard in the throat.

That was Ned's cue. He tore out of the room and through a crowd mingling at the entranceway. His feet hit the pavement on 11th Avenue and he kept running.

Defying oncoming cars and trucks, he ran across the six lanes and down 38th Street, stopping only to allow a fire truck to pull out in front of him. He flew over the bridge over 10th Avenue, finally stopping at the corner of 38th and Ninth. Traffic was at a standstill, and Ned spotted an empty cab. He jumped in and told the driver to take him to where he had parked the Indian. "It may take a while," said the driver. "And this is a one-way going downtown. I'm gonna have to take 11th back uptown."

"No!" Ned shouted, which startled the driver. "Don't take 11th," he said more calmly. "I just came from there—some kind of big ruckus at the Javits, tons of cop cars and everything."

"Okay, you're the boss," said the driver. "I can get you where you want to go, but it's gonna cost ya."

Chapter Fourteen

Even with the sun down for two hours now, it was still ridiculously hot. Ned had long since grown tired of the jokes the "coyotes"—professional border crossers—were making about a white guy trying to get *into* Mexico. They were sitting in a pickup truck in southern Pima County, Arizona, among the sparse brush and occasional saguaro. The thin, goateed guy in the passenger seat was scanning the horizon to the south with night-vision goggles and chatting casually with the driver in Spanish.

The two other "coyotes" were in the bed with Ned. They had grown tired of ribbing him and were biding their time, chatting in Spanish and occasionally playing cards. Both had gray t-shirts advertising American products, bright baseball caps doing the same and faded jeans. Ned had been introduced to the older one, Hilario, a day earlier.

He had driven from New York to Sahuarita, Arizona, just south of Tucson on the Indian. By staying off major highways and staying in dirt-bag, cash-only motels, he evaded police. After hours of riding through nothing but desert, Sahuarita appeared out of nowhere like a giant lushly verdant oasis. As he got closer, he saw that the sea of green was actually a well-manicured grove of broad-leafed pecan trees. Ned knew it was the result of some irrigation scheme, but it still struck him as odd, like a city in the middle of an ocean.

He went to the address on the card Andersson had provided him, passing by a bunch of auto service places and one hipster-style coffee shop. It was a low, faux Spanish-style adobe building in front and a painted metal warehouse behind. The receptionist took him into a back office and asked him to wait. He could hear the hum of the air conditioner and noticed that after riding in 110-degree heat, he felt almost cold inside. After about ten minutes, the man whose name was on the card, Harry Lucas, walked in and sat in the big leather chair behind the big but cheap-looking desk.

Lucas was a small, red-faced and gray-haired curmudgeon who wore jeans, a light-blue cowboy shirt and a huge black cowboy hat. He told Ned that "air conditioning is king" in Arizona, and that he "had outsmarted the Swede" by making his coils just across the border in Mexico. It was just as cheap as where the Swede got his and was just an hour's truck ride away.

Lucas listened to Ned's story. Then he laughed. "How does the Swede think I'm gonna make any money helping some chickenshit biker—no offense intended, of course—run away from the Russians?" he said. "And don't let him tell you I still owe him for that business up there in Canada—I paid him back plenty for that, too much. Sorry, son, I can't help you."

Ned could tell from the way Lucas stared at him that he was just holding out for some kind of payment. He didn't have a lot of cash left and was afraid to use his debit or credit cards. After some negotiations, Lucas offered to help get him over the border and even set him up at his factory on the other side. "The work is hard, mostly getting the lazy ones to do their jobs," said Lucas. "But I'll pay you almost American wages—and you won't have to worry about taxes. I'll get you papers and everything."

All he wanted in return was the Indian. Ned hated to part with it again, but knew that he had no choice. And anyway, he was much better off without a stolen motorcycle or any other key to link him to a previous identity. Lucas knew it was stolen, but said he knew enough people who could put it right again. He hated that Viking on the tank, though. Ned was about to agree and describe the Indian's original paint scheme and suggest where to buy the proper colors online, but Lucas interjected before he could speak. "That old-timey shit's no good," he said, more to himself than Ned. "Needs something natural—like a pronghorn or a sidewinder."

Ned handed Lucas the keys and warned him there might be a set or two in Delaware. Lucas said he wasn't worried and offered to take Ned out for dinner to seal the bargain and to introduce him to some friends.

The next evening Ned found himself in the bed of an old pickup truck parked in the scrubland outside the American town of Nogales, across the border from his destination—the huge industrial city of Heroica Nogales in Mexico. While Ned didn't relish the thought of spending the rest of his life in a Mexican factory, it was abundantly clear that he had worn out his welcome in the United States. Staying in his own country was tantamount to suicide.

The guy in the passenger seat put his goggles down and said something to the guys in back. They stood up and Hilario said "let's go" to Ned and handed him a backpack. The three jumped out of the pickup and ran, crouched low to avoid detection all the way to the border fence nearly a quarter-mile away. When they arrived, Hilario and his friend, Raul, pulled aside a loose section of mesh and crawled into Mexico. Ned followed.

He was mildly surprised that the other side of the border looked exactly the same as Arizona. The trio sprinted to another waiting pickup—same model, different color—jumped into the bed and held on as the driver started gathering speed over the bumpy dirt road.

Ned looked up. Raul was grinning at him. "What's with him?" Ned asked Hilario.

Hilario muttered something to Raul in Spanish. Then he turned back to Ned and flashed the same grin. "He says you are not here to run the factory."

"Oh yeah?" Ned looked at them both.

"Yeah, Raul says you are a bad man," Hilario said, and then leaned in closer. "You know, there are lots of ways outside of the factory to make money in Mexico."

Ned laughed to himself. "I'm listening," he said.

Biker
by Jerry Langton

The first book in the Ned Aiken series, featuring his life in the criminal biker brotherhood.

You'll never meet the bikers in this book or visit the mythical rust-belt city of Springfield. But through the eyes of Ned "Crash" Aiken, you will experience the real world of the outlaw biker gang—a world shaped by desperation, casual brutality and fascinating rites of passage. *Biker* follows the career trajectory of "Crash" from his days as a small-time high school drug dealer to his rapid rise through the ranks of a biker gang that is rapidly and brutally expanding its territory and criminal connections.

Aiken's story relates how an outlaw biker sees his gang from the inside. It is an experience shaped by seamy and ruthless characters waging a never-ending battle to establish their supremacy. From drug running and gun sales, to prostitution and allegiances forged by violence, this is a struggle played out within biker gangs the world over. And as the reader discovers in this intense docu-drama, this is not the romantic freewheeling beer-fest version of the Hells Angels, but a sleazy existence that draws social outcasts like moths to a flame.

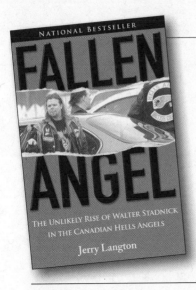

NATIONAL BESTSELLER

FALLEN ANGEL

THE UNLIKELY RISE OF WALTER STADNICK
IN THE CANADIAN HELLS ANGELS
Jerry Langton

Fallen Angel
by Jerry Langton

The unlikely rise of
Walter Stadnick in the
Canadian Hells Angels

Walter Stadnick is not an imposing man. At five-foot-four, his face
and arms scarred by fire in a motorcycle accident, he would not
spring to mind as a leader of Canada's most notorious biker gang,
the Hells Angels. Yet through sheer guts and determination, intel-
ligence and luck, this Hamilton-born youth rose in the Hells Angels
ranks to become national president. Not only did he lead the Angels
through the violent war with their rivals, the Rock Machine, in
Montreal in the Nineties, Stadnick saw opportunity to grow the
Hells Angels into a national criminal gang. He was a visionary—and
a highly successful one.

As Stadnick's influence spread, law enforcement took notice
of the Angel's growing presence in Ontario, Manitoba and British
Columbia. However, Stadnick's success did not come without a
price. Arrested and charged with 13 counts of first-degree murder,
Stadnick beat the murder charges but was convicted of gangsterism
and is currently serving time.

Fallen Angel details one man's improbable rise to power in one
of the world's most violent organizations, while shedding light on
how this enigmatic and dangerous biker gang operated and why it
remains so powerful.

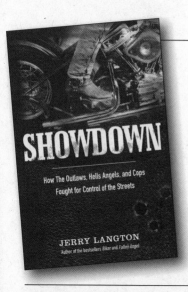

SHOWDOWN

How The Outlaws, Hells Angels, and Cops
Fought for Control of the Streets

JERRY LANGTON
Author of the bestsellers *Biker* and *Fallen Angel*

Showdown
by Jerry Langton

Control of Ontario's underworld
wasn't decided in a day, a year,
or any single event. It was a
series of skirmishes, bloodbaths
and blunders.

When the old-school Mafia in Hamilton fell apart following the
death of Johnny "Pops" Papalia, a frenzy ensued for who would
control Ontario's drug and vice traffic. The leader of the Hells
Angels, Walter Stadnick, had had his eye on Canada's most lucrative drug market for years but had been kept out largely due to the
mafia syndicate that only reluctantly employed bikers of any stripe
for their dirty work, and Papalia's refusal to use any Hells Angels.

The war to fill the power vacuum in Ontario would hinge on
the broadly supported Stadnick's Hells Angels, a handful of smaller
clubs too proud or too useless to join them, and Mario "The Wop"
Parente's Outlaws, the top motorcycle club in Ontario since the 70s.
Other challengers would emerge from the ever-shifting allegiances
of the biker world, including the Bandidos from south of the border, whose presence in the province would end in a bloodbath now
known as the Shedden Massacre. Against all of these competing
interests stood the various law enforcement agencies responsible
for keeping the general peace and shutting down as many opera-
tions as they could.

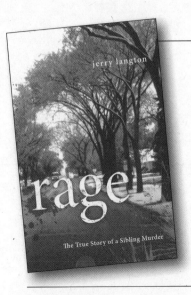

Rage
by Jerry Langton

Sibling violence may be as old as
time, but this case is particularly
disturbing and unsettling.

In a quiet working-class neighborhood in east-end Toronto, on an
early winter day in November 2003, Johnathon Madden returned
home from school only to be bullied and threatened by his older
brother, Kevin; Kevin's friend Tim Ferriman; and another teenager.
The confrontation turned violent and fatal. Johnathon didn't have
the strength or size to protect himself against the frenzied attack of
his powerful 250-pound brother.

Kevin Madden had problems. This was not news to his family, teachers, principal, social workers, and psychiatrists. But what
drove him to commit murder—and why Johnathon? Why were his
friends compelled to take part in the bloodletting? What events
were going on behind the scenes that played a part in the tragedy?

Jerry Langton sets out to answer these questions and look for
the clues that drove Kevin Madden over the edge. His investigation
takes him onto the streets of Toronto, where he unearths a disturbing teen subculture, into cyberspace, and into the confidence of
neighbors and students who knew the Madden family. Langton
reveals shocking testimony from the trials—one of which was declared a mistrial due to the perjury of a witness—and exposes the
twisted lives of youth living in a parallel universe where death is
met with complacency.

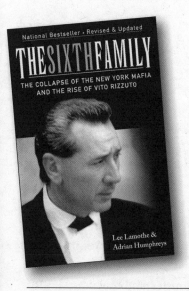

The Sixth Family
by Lee Lamothe &
Adrian Humphreys

"A briskly written and timely story of the rise and apparent fall of the Rizzuto crime family in Montreal, with enough blam-blam to keep true crime buffs turning the pages."

—*The National Post*

"[*The Sixth Family*] is essential reading, not only in the context of the looming Rizzuto murder trial, but for anyone concerned about the intrusion of traditional organized crime into every facet of our society."

—*The Globe and Mail*

"With a reporter's eye for detail and a novelist's gift for storytelling, the two authors lay bare the Rizzuto family's inner workings and international connections."

—*The Record* (Kitchener)

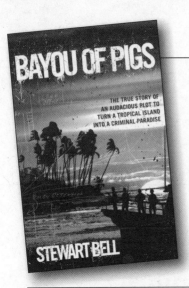

THE TRUE STORY OF
AN AUDACIOUS PLOT TO
TURN A TROPICAL ISLAND
INTO A CRIMINAL-PARADISE

STEWART BELL

Bayou of Pigs
by Stewart Bell

The true story about an
idyllic tropical island and the
mercenaries who set out to
steal if for profit and adventure.

In 1981, a small but heavily armed force of misfits from the United
States and Canada set off on a preposterous mission to invade an
impoverished Caribbean country, overthrow its government in a
coup d'état, install a puppet prime minister, and transform it into
a crooks' paradise.

Their leader was a Texas soldier-of-fortune type named Mike
Perdue. His lieutenant was a Canadian Nazi named Wolfgang
Droege. Their destination: Dominica.

For two years they recruited fighting men, wooed investors,
stockpiled weapons, and forged links with the mob, leftist revo-
lutionaries, and militant Rastafarians. They called their invasion
Operation Red Dog. They were going to make millions. People were
going to die. An entire nation was going to suffer. All that stood in
their way were two federal agents from New Orleans on the biggest
case of their lives.

Set in the Caribbean, Canada, and the American South at the
beginning of the end of the Cold War, and based on hundreds of
pages of declassified US government documents as well as exclu-
sive interviews with those involved, *Bayou of Pigs* tells a remarkable
tale of foreign military intervention, revolutionary politics, greed,
treachery, stupidity, deceit, and one of the most outlandish criminal stunts ever conceived: the theft of a nation.

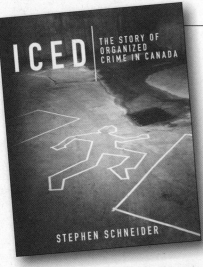

Iced
by Stephen Schneider

"You're lucky he didn't have
an ice pick in his hands.
I know how this guy
performs."

> — *Mobster Paul Volpe speaking about a Buffalo-mafia enforcer named "Cicci"*

Iced: The Story of Organized Crime in Canada is a remarkable parallel history to the one generally accepted and taught in our schools. Organized crime has had a significant impact on the shaping of this country and the lives of its people. The most violent and thuggish—outlaw motorcycle gangs like the Hells Angels—have been exalted to mythic proportions. The families who owned distilleries during Prohibition, such as the Bronfmans, built vast fortunes that today are vested in corporate holdings. The mafia in Montreal created and controlled the largest heroin and cocaine smuggling empire in the world, feeding the insatiable appetite of our American neighbors. Today, gangs are laying waste the streets of Vancouver, and "BC bud" flows into the U.S. as the marijuana of choice.

Comprehensive, informative and entertaining, *Iced* is a romp across the nation and across the centuries. In these pages you will meet crime groups that are at once sordid and inept, yet resourceful entrepreneurs and self-proclaimed champions of the underdog, who operate in full sight of their communities and the law. This is the definitive book on organized crime in Canada, and a unique contribution to our understanding of Canadian history.

Jerry Langton has written for *The Hamilton Spectator* and *Maclean's*, and worked for *The Daily News* in New York. He is a freelance writer whose articles appear in *The Globe and Mail*, *Toronto Star* and *National Post*. Langton's the author of the bestseller *Fallen Angel: The Unlikely Rise of Walter Stadnick in the Canadian Hells Angels*; *Showdown: How the Outlaws, Hells Angels, and Cops Fought for Control of the Streets*; *Biker: Inside the Notorious World of an Outlaw Motorcycle Gang*; and *Rage: The True Story of a Sibling Murder*.